Born in Italy of Hungarian parents, Inez Baranay migrated to the western suburbs of Sydney, where she was educated, then moved to the inner city. She has been a schoolteacher, traveller, compulsive shopper, televisi~ ~~~~~~~~~~~~ ~ journalist. Her short stories l  anthologies. Her first novel, of travel stories, *The Saddes* in 1989. She lives in Sydney.

Also by Inez Baranay
and available in Imprint

Between Careers
The Saddest Pleasure

IMPRINT

PAGAN

INEZ BARANAY

ANGUS
& ROBERTSON

Arts for Australians

Australia | **Council**

*Collins/Angus & Robertson Publishers'
creative writing programme is assisted by
the Australia Council, the Australian
government's arts advisory and support
organisation.*

AN ANGUS & ROBERTSON BOOK

*First published in Australia in 1990 by
Collins/Angus & Robertson Publishers Australia*

*Collins/Angus & Robertson Publishers Australia
Unit 4, Eden Park, 31 Waterloo Road, North Ryde
NSW 2113, Australia*

*William Collins Publishers Ltd
31 View Road, Glenfield, Auckland 10, New Zealand*

*Angus & Robertson (UK)
16 Golden Square, London W1R 4BN, United Kingdom*

*National Library of Australia
Cataloguing-in-Publication data:*

*Baranay, Inez.
  Pagan.
  ISBN 0 207 16681 1.
  I.Title.
A823.3*

Cover illustration: Black Magic *by Rosaleen Norton*

*Typeset in 11pt Times Roman by Midland Typesetters, Victoria
Printed in Australia by Globe Press*

5   4   3   2   1
95   94   93   92   91   90

to my mother and my father

ACKNOWLEDGEMENTS

My thanks to Renee Goossens for her generous support. Renee's memoir, *Facing the Music*, was an important starting point for this book. For helpful suggestions thanks to Gil Appleton and Sasha Soldatow, Tom Thompson and Nikki Christer of Collins/A&R, and Barbara Mobbs. And always thanks to Milena Quansah.

Interviews, conversations and correspondence with many people were an enormous help. My thanks to Keith Adam, Werner Baer, Helen Bainton, Nancy Borlase, Lindsay Browne, Betsy Brown, Tex Clarke, Nevill Drury, Merle Everard, Margaret Fink, Charmian Gadd, Walter Glover, Richard Goldner, Hayes Gordon, Richard Hall, Laura Hopkins, Ilse Huber, John Kingsmill, Martin Long, Jock McKenna, Paul Maclay, Frank Mitchell, Joe Morris, Sir Charles Moses, Elizabeth Riddell, Marianne Rogala-Koczorovski, Julian Russell, Jean Salmon, Sidonie Scott, A. H. Trevener, Peter Sainthill, Lex Watson, John West and Bill Wright.

'We have difficulties in finding the silence
from which music then emerges . . .'

PROLOGUE

THIRTY YEARS LATER

'He was a great conductor. He came here after the war. He was a tremendous force in Sydney's—and Australia's—musical and cultural life. He introduced modern music, he brought world standards, he made the orchestra great. People forget that. All they know is the scandal.'

'He was a victim of a parochial, puritanical society. Whatever that stuff was he was caught with, it'd be mild by today's standards, it'd be nothing, something you could get at the corner newsagent's.'

'That conductor—when he was here, Australia made recordings for the rest of the world. We never did anything for the rest of the world before.'

'He was obviously set up. He was framed.'

'There are powerful people in this town who are into very serious, very heavy black magic, they obtain placentas from hospitals, they obtain bones from morgues, and they don't want anything found out about what they do and if you ask too many questions you'll wind up in trouble, hexed, dead. Take my advice and drop this whole thing. Leave it alone. Write about something else.'

'We knew him very well, or thought we did. We had no idea what he was involved in. It was an immense shock to everyone. We never saw him again. He left. Then he died.'

'Someone saw him in London, after he had to leave here. They said he was a man encased in ice.'

'It was probably some jealous tuba player.'

'My dear, we all know who it was, look at who gained. Who took his place?'

'He was a great man, treated abominably. No one came to his defence.'

'He was into pederasty and black magic.'

'He was writing monthly cheques to a certain person for the rest of his life.'

'Only one person came to his defence.'

'These days, people would say "so what?". No one said that then. Not in public. Not in time.'

'There were threats, he couldn't tell the truth about why he was framed.'

'I could never get to the bottom of it, and you won't either.'

'It is better left alone, better forgotten.'

MARCH 1956

VON KRONEN CHECK photos seized VICE MEN ACT—CIB Gets
World Calls SUMMONS SOON FOR VON K Lady von K living
at Paris convent VON KRONEN FACES INDECENT PICTURES
CHARGE—TALKS TO *MAIL* VON KRONEN FAILS TO APPEAR
IN COURT Hearing Put Off—Secret Report on von Kronen
Tomorrow GIVES UP HIS TWO BIG JOBS—Von Kronen Case—
WORLD FIGURE—PARTY IS PUT OFF VON K MAY NOT
APPEAR Too Ill To Go To Court VON K CASE OFF FOR A
WEEK VON KRONEN GUILTY—Maximum £100 fine imposed
THREATS ALLEGED GUILTY VERDICT: VON K CASE Pictures
Result of Threats, says counsel. Books in Suitcase Crowds Jammed
Corridors VON K BLACKMAIL STORY CONDUCTOR WILL
LEAVE POST Board to Decide on von Kronen's Job VON KRONEN
WON'T RETAIN MUSIC POST

1

THE THUNDERSTORM

Sydney, 1917

When she was born she caused a thunderstorm. There were floods in the town. She would have known she was born in a storm, even if they had not told her. She must be born portentously, she must be announced. She, who loved the night and darkness, determined very early that thunderbolts and lightning would storm again at her command.

No one remembers their birth, they say. They say, they say, she would think in scornful fury. She remembered that dance of energies, the whirling cosmos. She remembered that, and before that.

That night, her mother told her, when you were born, and little Evie took up her crayons and began with a bright zig-zag across the page, and there was the endless sky where nature danced her passion, stamped and whirled and wailed, her eyes flashed and sparks flew from her heels and Eveleen burst forth. Such pain, and I nearly died, her mother said. In a tiny town in a distant nation thunder announced her and the window panes rattled; she sucked life into herself, the rain wept and the gutters filled up and overflowed.

Then the lightning flashed.

Layers of thick drapes were drawn against the world. The room smelt of dust. She was hung by the heels and dealt a hefty blow. She bellowed in fury and they smiled.

And the thunderstorm blew itself out over the sea. Out there, out at sea, her father looked over his charts on a big Navy ship that was going to war.

The cat from next-door would come to sit with her and she would look into its pulsating slanted eyes. When she was one, the cat scratched her, deliberately, drawing three thin lines of

1

bright red blood. She felt a thrill. Then her mother suddenly materialised, clucking and fussing, so alarmed that her baby had been hurt. That naughty naughty cat, did you pull its tail and hurt poor kitty? A kiss to make it better and something wet and stinging on the arm in case of germs. Evie cried, but not because of the pain.

Her mother, with nanny standing by the door, wanted her to play with the toys. Mother knelt, Mother begged. Play with dolly; dolly is your baby; Mummy loves Evie and Evie loves dolly. I'm drawing, said Eveleen. The stupid pink rubber pretend human baby, she threw the wretched thing across the room.

When her mother had gone, Eveleen took up the crayon and remembered the scratch on her arm and began to draw. What is that, Evie? the big sisters said. A nothing. Looks like a funny kind of goat, or pig. It was shaped like a cloud, with long arms that were reaching and bending all over, and its head was a bit like a wolf or a bit like a lynx.

Eveleen, said the mother and held it out to her. It was a biscuit, her mother wanted her to eat it. No, I don't want it, said Eveleen. You don't say no when Mummy gives you a biscuit, you say thank you, Mummy. No, she said. Where's the please and thank you? demanded the mother. Take the nice bikkie, say thank you and eat it. No, said Eveleen, and felt the blow on her face. For a moment there was only sharp red pain. Then Eveleen screamed.

The mother said she must eat the nice biscuit and took hold of little Eveleen and pushed the biscuit into her mouth, to teach her not to say no like that. The sugary floury thing, she spat it out. Then the slap and then hate—didn't her mother understand that Evie could never be made to? So Evie was so sick that her stomach heaved and triumphantly she brought up all the things she had eaten long before the biscuit. Her mother suddenly had a raging fever and had to stay in bed for a week.

Evie wanted to stay home to sleep by day. Even at the age of four she did not want to sleep at night. When they all said 'good night' she yelled and stamped. Good night, good night!

2

The night was good, yes, good for watching the world all shadows and shades; good for sitting at the window and listening to the darkness. 'Good night!' Let *them* go to bed, let them *leave* her to the night, her own dear sinister night.

And then the teacher. At drawing she walked round the room and looked over the shoulders and stopped behind Evie. 'That's not how a cat goes,' she said. 'Here,' and she took the crayon from Eveleen who had already been drawing forever. 'It's not a cat!' said Evie. 'Oh, it looks a bit like a cat. What is it? And is this one an octopus?' 'It's a nothing.' 'Oh, everything has a name,' said the teacher. 'What is its name?' 'Nothing, it's a *nothing*,' said little Evie, angry now. 'Do you want to draw a real cat?' said the teacher. 'NO!' screamed Eveleen, her face hot and red, her eyes wet. 'No!' she screamed, and she threw all her crayons onto the floor. The teacher couldn't speak, she had lost her voice for the rest of the day.

And Eveleen, although she had been named for the heroine of a pink-covered romance, proudly took her rightful place as the bad girl. Sometimes the other children would follow her. Don't do that, Eveleen told them and they would not. Do this, she said, and they did it. The teacher always knew that Evie had made them, and Evie always took the blame. She did not like other children, they wanted to be led and never blamed; they brought presents for the teacher: a flower picked on the way to school, a cake their mother had made, a picture postcard from an aunt in England. They would beam at the teacher as they held these things out: aren't I good? The other children did not like her, Eveleen knew, but they always did what she told them, often enough anyway, and that was better than liking her, which would have been of no use at all.

At home the big sisters brought her lots of coloured pencils and paper. Do a drawing, they said, do another nothing.

Next-door's cat came and sat in the window. Evie drew the best nothing-beast ever: it moved and danced around the page and Evie chased it with her pens, finding its shapes and colours. The cat blinked at her and the nothing writhed on her page,

3

and between its legs was stuck a thing like she'd seen on dogs in the street. Evie coloured the thing purple and it grew up out of the beast and then she fell to the floor with her head ringing burning pain and the mother crying and scolding: bad bad Evie, horrible drawing horrible cat. And she shooed the cat away. Later Evie made more of these drawings.

Then a year after school started, so she was six, she woke in her little bed. Beside her was the shiningest beast there ever was. She had never seen one like this, its scales like goldy-green jewels. It was standing like a lizard, like a cat, like a scaly bear, but also it shone and shimmered. There was no sound—not only no sound, but the normal faint noises she could hear when she listened hard on a quiet night awake and alone were not there—so it was no-no-sound all around and it stood and shimmered by her bed, come there so she would know they really existed, and sometimes could be seen.

Later she found that this beast was called a dragon, and that people say that dragons 'do not exist'. It had a name, and there were pictures of dragons (though none so still and luminous as hers). And yet *they say* that these pictured, named beings do not exist! They say! Eveleen knew that she had seen the dragon, she knew she would see her dragon again, and stranger creatures too. She knew she would draw them, these creatures. She knew she would create even greater pictures to horrify mothers and teachers. She knew that her life forever was connected with affirming the existence of denied beings.

2
THAT DISAPPOINTING DAY

It felt all wrong, how quiet it had been that night. The chops had been kept warm for his tea, the radio had been on in the kitchen and soon he would go to bed. 'Tomorrow you'd hear about it, though,' he had consoled himself. 'You'd hear plenty more tomorrow, for sure.'

When Detective-Sergeant Trevor Thomas thought of that disappointing day in March 1956, he got angry. He had expected to be celebrating at the end of that day; for the rest of his life, in fact. He had expected pats on the back. Thirty years later, he was still waiting for them.

'The abominable crime of buggery' was the only crime in Australia's law books to be blessed with its own adjective.

'I had the proof I needed,' he would say, telling his story. Still, he hadn't been able to make his arrest, and had been so close to it, and that was why it had turned out a gravely disappointing day. He had achieved a fantastic result then hadn't been able to get the warrant he needed. An arrest like that would have made his career. He had worked hard on the case, and then he'd been sabotaged. That's what he said. The people higher up were looking after each other.

At the end of that day, Trevor Thomas sipped his beer while the wife did the washing-up. She had the radio going in the kitchen. She'd told him that the news had been on the radio all day. She wasn't sure where she had heard of the man they'd caught, then Joyce next-door reminded her that he was the one with the American wife who always used to be in the social pages. 'Remember her piled-up hair in the Sunday papers,' his wife said from the kitchen.

It should have been a day of great triumph: the mighty fallen, the high-and-mighty vanquished. And so he was. The Maestro was back that night in his north shore home with a pretty good idea by now, and all housewives in their kitchens, and even their relaxing hubbies, would agree that you didn't get away with things like that here. Not in Australia. 'Whatever they get up to over there,' Thomas muttered. He thought about how he could get hold of some of the pictures that were found that day. You could show a few people how twisted some of these foreign types really were, being let into the country, corrupting the young, encouraging poofters and perverts, destroying morals and decent standards, lowering the tone of the place.

It had all started a few days back. The case had started a few months ago, but a few days back Trevor Thomas had received his information. He didn't ask where Col had got it from, didn't want to know. The important thing was that he knew the subject was due to leave London on March 8 and would arrive at Kingsford Smith at 8 a.m. the next day.

Thomas was then granted his conference with Victor Mould, the head of the Vice Squad. Mould made it clear he wanted Thomas to do whatever he could. They wouldn't ask too many questions about where he got his information. And Thomas wouldn't ask too many questions about why they were so keen. Mould hinted that there would be much pleasure higher up if it was successful, and Thomas could expect his future preferences to be looked on with favour. It was clear to him that the higher ups were keen on a big coup, something to show how vigilant they were, keeping Australia clean, free from dirty foreign influences.

The next step was to call Inspector Darren Wilder, the top bloke in Customs.

'I've got a tip-off. It's a big one,' Detective-Sergeant Thomas told him. 'Things involved you wouldn't even be able to tell your wife.'

'Really? What more can you tell me?'

'Nothing more at this stage, but I'll need your most senior man.'

'If it's that big,' said Wilder, 'I'll come myself.'

'I'll meet you at the airport at seven a.m.'

'You don't want to tell me who it is?' But the detective had hung up.

Then Thomas had to find someone from Police to accompany him. 'It's a big one,' he said again, with emphatic gravity, to the men at the station. 'I can't say who.' They all turned to water at the mention of a Knight of the Realm; suddenly everyone had something else to do, or it was their day off. 'A bloody big one,' said Constable Witcher, as he closed his locker. 'If you make one slip or your luck's against you, you'll be out in one-horse Woop-Woop for the rest of your days.'

Lucky there was Bingo Lipps from the Balmain shop. 'I'm not doing anything tomorrow. I'm keen. I'll have a go.'

'I'm not telling you any more for now,' said Thomas. 'I pick you up at five-thirty and we go to the airport.'

'Fair enough.'

Darren Wilder, the Customs bloke, was waiting at the airport, all right. 'Right,' Trevor Thomas said, 'this is what's happening. Just get him called over to Customs.'

Wilder whistled when he heard the name. 'Hope you're sure of yourself.'

'No worries there. And don't tell him I'm police,' Thomas told Wilder.

Thomas didn't want to tell him who he was first up. He wanted to watch him get nabbed, watch him crumple.

When the Qantas flight landed they were all ready. Sir Eduard von Kronen was one of the first off the plane. Down the steps, that long stride of his along the tarmac, his velour-collared big black overcoat worn over his shoulders like a cloak, black velour hat worn to one side, his briefcase ('that's the briefcase,' said Thomas) in one hand. There was an outbreak of applause from a bunch of admirers waiting for him.

Some of them waited until the end, Thomas was told later.

'Here's a bet that none of them will ever own up to even being there,' he replied.

Detective-Sergeant Trevor Thomas stood at the entrance to the Customs hall. All the passengers would have to pass through there, go right past him. Von Kronen caught his glance, and as he passed him and caught his look he bestowed a grand nod of the head, even a 'how'd'y'do'. Trevor got a real kick out of recounting that one.

Then over the loudspeaker: 'Would Sir Eduard von Kronen please go up to the medical room.' The medical room was the only place available for questioning people. Kingsford Smith in those days was a very small airport.

They were waiting for him. Von Kronen came in, aloof and arrogant, holding his briefcase. He would have been wondering, Thomas knew, if this was where they left messages, if someone from his family was sick.

Wilder came up to him and introduced himself. 'Do you have anything to declare, Sir Eduard? Anything else, anything you haven't declared?'

'No,' said von Kronen, looking quite unperturbed. He was cool, all right.

'May I ask what is in your briefcase?'

'Music, musical scores, naturally.'

'May I see?'

The briefcase he was carrying would never before have been searched. Von Kronen only raised his eyebrows coolly. 'Yes, of course, but the briefcase is locked.'

'Would you unlock it please, sir.'

Von Kronen raised his eyebrows again and stood still for a second. Then he began to fumble in his pockets for the key.

'Talk about a woman's handbag stuffed with rubbish!' Trevor would later report. Out of his waistcoat came bits of string, erasers, papers, pens, fumble, fumble, looks like he can't quite find his key, so of course the gentlemen will wave him on and that will be that. That's what he thought.

Wilder produced a penknife with a big, mean, curved blade

8

on it and said, quite pleasantly, 'I'm afraid that in the absence of a key I will have to open the briefcase by force.' It didn't take much more fumbling for the key to be found.

The briefcase was opened. Trevor Thomas was watching the back of von Kronen's neck, the white shirt and blue collar. The collar became damp.

In the briefcase there were the musical scores, five of them. Wilder picked one up. 'What's this?'

' "Carmina Burana",' Sir Eduard answered. 'Carl Orff. A scenic oratorio. They're playing a lot of it in Europe. I thought we'd do it here this season.'

Wilder was looking at the way the sheets of music had been taped together on all four sides.

'The words come from student poems from a Bavarian monastery of the thirteenth century. The piece however is quite *moderne.*'

'That right?' said Wilder.

'It's quite interesting the first time you hear it.' You could see why he kept talking.

Wilder used his knife to slit open the tape. There were envelopes taped inside. The envelopes were sealed. Wilder slit one open. He took out a pile of photographs and fanned them out and looked at them. His face set; he was obviously controlling himself; he could not allow himself to whistle, or gasp, or laugh. Wilder did not look at anyone as he opened the next envelope. And looked inside. And the next.

Then he put all the photographs back in the envelopes and said, 'Bring in the rest of his luggage.'

'There must be,' said Sir Eduard, 'a telephone I can use.' His question was never answered. 'Look,' he said, accustomed to deference, 'I have a driver outside. People are waiting for me.'

'I'm sorry, sir, you'll have to wait.'

'Look,' the conductor said, 'I can't keep the driver waiting. Appointments . . . meetings . . . a tight schedule.'

But they all turned to the luggage.

In the luggage, there were expensive English clothes—

cashmere sweaters, shirts of finest linen, suits of wool, glossy leather shoes; there were more musical scores, with more strange titles and queer names on the cream, grey and beige front covers. And there were more of *those* things: books, films, photographs, incense, and some weird-looking masks that weren't meant for a kiddies' birthday party.

And there was the medal among it all. Trevor Thomas basked in a moment of glorious self-vindicating outrage. 'I'm a Royalist,' he would always explain, proudly. 'I mean, you get those commo types who say "who does it hurt",' he was to say to the men he trusted from the shop. 'And this bloke will come in with his knighthood stuck in among a bunch of dirty filthy pictures.'

'Who's conning who?' grumbled his mates.

'That's right. That's exactly right,' he replied.

'They'd let people bring any bloody thing into the country,' they grumbled.

'No idea. They've got no idea.'

'Give's another look,' said the old sergeant, reaching for the souvenir that Wilder had slipped Thomas.

'They've come up to me, people have,' Trevor Thomas related, 'and said, you shouldn't have done it, he's done so much for music. Done a lot of harm, too, though. Trying to recruit people into this stuff.'

'Aw they do,' the men said. 'They try and get the young ones in.'

'Yair,' said Thomas. 'After all that, I was told to drop the whole thing. All *he* ever got was a fine for the importation.'

And for Thomas that should have been only a preliminary, only a step towards the big arrest for indecent assault, the arrest he had been waiting so long to make. He had proof! But while he was still in the medical room at the airport, while Wilder was taking offending items out of the costly pigskin bags, while the conductor was protesting that he had naturally not packed his own bags (his valet had done that), they were to go to find the valet (who was in London, of course) and ask the valet about these things; the valet would know why they were there. While all that was going on, Trevor Thomas began to find out that things had stopped turning out the way he had planned.

Victor Mould, the Vice Squad chief, had rung the first time when the luggage was being brought in. 'Can't really talk now,' Thomas had muttered into the phone, 'but Wilder is definitely onto something here.'

Then Mould had rung again. 'I'm on my way out. Hang on till I get there.'

Trevor Thomas would never know who Mould had spoken to in the interval. Mould took over when he arrived, and that was official. Now that Customs had got involved, they had no choice but to proceed with the questioning, and would take Sir Eduard down to the Criminal Investigation Bureau. But Thomas would not be questioning him over any further matters. Trevor Thomas had done a good job—he knew he had, and even the Commissioner of Police was to tell him so, and the Commissioner was not known for using many words of praise. But even the Commissioner could be given orders.

Trevor Thomas was to say that if von Kronen ever came back into the country—and he really hoped he would—he would arrest him then, a citizen's arrest. He still had the evidence. He kept it for the rest of his life. He had made copies of his reports, and had kept one inside the wheel of his car, one at home, one in his locker.

Anyway, they had all regretted, the Commissioner and the Chief and Lipps, that it couldn't be taken further, Detective-Sergeant Trevor Thomas knew that. But Thomas would never get the warrant he needed to make the arrest on the indecency charge. His evidence was to be shelved, his report was to vanish, the file destroyed.

He knew for sure that it was not all going to go his way when they left that medical room. During that morning, Thomas had thought of Col O'Brien waiting patiently out there on his own; he was the kind you could count on to wait, he was waiting for the scoop of his life, and Thomas hoped he had got a photographer to wait with him, and a snapshot would be taken.

11

But when they walked out of the airport, the Inspector of Customs, the head of the Vice Squad, the two policemen and the conductor, they did not walk past one newsman and one photographer; they walked straight into a blinding flash of white light.

3
BLEW THE EXCLUSIVE

March 1956

Col O'Brien called his editor early. Very early. 'I can't tell you any more than this, I've got an exclusive, and it's a big one. Hold the front page.'

'Listen, Col,' the editor drawled, 'I don't want to fill the front page with advertisements again.'

'You won't, bloody oath you won't. Get a photographer down to CIB . . .'

'Why don't you tell me all about it.'

'No time. Trust me. A photographer at CIB, tell him to look out for car AOK A38, that's Detective-Sergeant Thomas's car. Photograph him and anyone with him. Got that? Believe me, this is a big one . . .'

The editor shrugged and rang a reporter who was down at CIB. He passed on the instructions, told him to get a photographer to wait for the car. No, he wasn't going to tell him why. The reporter, Mike Randell, was a senior reporter, and didn't like anyone knowing more than he did. He knew his way around, so he went up to see the chief of the CIB. The chief said, 'Don't ask me about it, Thomas isn't on my staff, he's on Mould's staff.' Randell found his way up to the office of Victor Mould. He knocked and went straight in.

'Where's Trevor Thomas today?' he asked. 'What's he doing today?'

Mould didn't like Randell, and he had a Big Shot on the line. 'Get out,' said Mould, 'or I'll throw you out. I'll throw you off the balcony.' He returned to the phone, and took orders. He was not to let things go any further. Mould telephoned the airport and found that they were still inspecting baggage. He told Trevor Thomas to keep things at a standstill till he

13

got there. Then he called for his car.

Mike Randell got more and more aggrieved, waiting and not knowing what was going on. So he kept wandering around and asking everyone loudly what they knew, whom they were expecting. Why were they going to photograph whoever was in Detective-Sergeant Thomas's car? No one knew. He had a bright idea. He remembered that Thomas was from Balmain police station, and so he rang up Balmain and they told him that Thomas wasn't there, he was at Mascot.

Randell wasn't the only reporter hanging round the station. There was Bill Hoskins, who was doing police rounds for the *Post*, and Hoskins heard all this, heard Randell asking for Thomas. Hoskins rang Balmain too. Detective-Sergeant Thomas was at Mascot, they told him, and Bill Hoskins went out to Mascot too, stopping only to call his editor. Before long some other newspapermen heard that their colleagues were rushing out to Mascot and they decided to take themselves out there too. Some thought they might get a free flight somewhere. You never know.

Detective-Sergeant Thomas's old mole, Col O'Brien, was already out at the airport, monitoring the time that was being spent in the medical room. A long time. He would have dearly loved to be in there. He paced around. He noticed the luggage being taken in. He watched the people who had come to meet the conductor off the plane. They argued among themselves, some left, some kept on waiting. More time passed. No one emerged from the medical room. He noted that they sent out for tea and sandwiches. Then an official police car arrived, and Victor Mould was in it. There really was something going on.

And then more cars arrived at the airport—and Col O'Brien swore. It was the others. The other bloody papers. And they kept on coming.

That blew the exclusive.

Lucky that in that mob there was a photographer from his own paper. The first photographs would be taken here, not at CIB.

The excitement built up, even though no one knew why. All

they knew was, it was some important bloke from overseas, and Customs had been questioning him for hours. Soon you couldn't get a phone call into or out of Australia, the papers were tying up the lines. It hadn't been like that since Evdokia Petrov defected. A lot of people were dead certain it was another espionage case, and said so, loudly.

Those music people who had come early to meet Sir Eduard and to applaud when he alighted from the plane were still there. They saw all the newspapermen arrive. They didn't want to talk to newspapermen, most of them. But the newspapermen found out that Eduard von Kronen had been called over the PA and hadn't emerged since. Talk went round. He was connected with some espionage investigation. He was defecting. He was helping someone defect. He had smuggled secret intelligence. He had intelligence planted on him. He was assisting police, assisting the Secret Service in its investigations.

Finally they emerged: Eduard von Kronen flanked by two plain-clothes police, followed by the head of the Vice Squad, and the top Customs official. Flash! All the cameramen got that one. He was allowed to say a few words. 'Everything is all right,' he said. 'I am just having a little discussion with these friends.'

The friends led him to their car, and the flash of photographers' lights followed them all the way. Pressmen followed them to CIB headquarters too, where more of them were waiting.

Von Kronen still looked like a man who couldn't believe he was in trouble. He obviously thought, soon it will be all right. This can't happen to me. Everything will be all right.

4
THE LAST CONCERT

October 1955

Sydney Town Hall was one of the grandest buildings in the city, with a frequently consulted clock tower that took the citizens' eyes to heaven. Erected in 1888, it was a stone edifice in the imposing style of Victorian public buildings. People who worked in town gathered on its broad stone steps to eat their lunchtime sandwiches in the sunshine. Mothers and their grown-up daughters put on their hats and gloves and met there, and old friends who went shopping together rang up and said, 'I'll meet you on the Town Hall steps.'

When the evenings were mild and fresh the tang of the harbour carried up George Street just as far as the Town Hall. Women in silk frocks and men in suits waiting to go inside congregated on the broad steps and told each other what a warm day it had been. Warm for October they said, summer is coming. Early spring days often are warm in Sydney, until a spell of cold winds later in October or November makes everyone say, 'Isn't summer late this year.' Not that you get a really cold winter here, some of the concert-goers remind each other. In London, in Vienna, we needed our furs, the snow, below-freezing.

Nora Ujhazy sat waiting on the wide stone balustrade along one side of the steps and Patrick Morris walked up George Street. They saw each other at the same moment. They smiled, smiles that said more than, 'Hello, so there you are,' smiles that sang 'you! you!'.

Smiles like that could cause a sharp stab in the breast of older people. 'Oh well,' said June Henry, 'we were young once,' but her husband had not seen the young couple's greeting, and he was not listening to her, and only lifted her slipping shawl up onto her shoulders, a gesture that pleased June for showing

16

an attentive husband, but also irritated her for its effeminate fussiness.

What a crowd. Capacity audience. The last concert of the season. 'Ten years ago,' Nigel Donne reminded them as the Henrys found themselves pressed up close to the Donnes, 'you wouldn't have had a dozen people here.'

Ten years ago the war was just ending and you still did not know quite how it would all turn out. It all turned out well. Now you could afford new shantung ensembles and a new Frigidaire at home. And subscriptions to concerts.

Before he had even entered the concert hall Nigel Donne made some mental notes for his review. It would be a summing-up of the season. He would mention that evidently there now was a bigger concert audience than Sydney had ever dreamed of. For things had changed.

Australian men wouldn't have been seen dead at a symphony concert, until the war. Australian girls had seen men carry flowers in the street, and had seen men go to concerts. And you couldn't say these American men were not men; they *were* men. And Australian men had gone away and some had come back changed. And the displaced people from Europe came to live here and, as they shook themselves out of bewilderment and pain and made a life, as they learned to stop making comparisons, as they buried the past and made a new future, they came to concerts and formed chamber music groups and bit by bit they began to enter the orchestra. And above all, there was Sir Eduard von Kronen. He had made headlines when he accepted his appointment to Sydney, for he was world-class and world-famous, and yet he chose to come here, not only as a touring guest conductor, as others had done, but to live here, to build up the orchestra and the School of Music. Sir Eduard came, and music became something to be written about in the papers.

Dimity Gette was making notes for her 'My Week' column in the *Mail*. She had her own job to do: her readers relied on her observations. Who was there and what were they wearing? And she would observe that Mrs von Kronen, Lady von Kronen,

17

had not been seen for . . . was it two years? Would she really be joining her husband in Europe? She did provide good copy, that Madeleine. She was the overbearing American: loud and brash. But you had to hand it to her, no one else could dress the way she did. What music would they play tonight? Dimity hoped for something nice and old-fashioned, something you could recognise. She knew she had better not talk about music. She'd ask June, and then put it in her own words, 'brilliant sound', that sort of thing.

'The migrant girls, you must admit . . .' June Henry was saying to Dimity Gette. And Dimity nodded, and made a note about their high cheekbones and lovely dark eyes and how they added colour and difference to our concert nights.

Nora, high-cheeked and dark-eyed, had been to the Town Hall to hear the orchestra more times than she could count. Usually it was for rehearsals. All the senior music students were encouraged to go to rehearsals. Tonight she had tickets to the actual concert.

'Come on!' she said, and led Patrick as they pushed and ducked and darted through the crowd on the steps, and they were right at the doors when they opened at the sound of the chimes. Behind them, the crowd fanned out from the narrow entrance to the wide lower steps that reached the footpath. People began to press up together in a long, slow procession.

Nora found their seats. Perhaps she should not have led the way so definitely, even though she had been here so many times and he had not. Would he like the concert? If not, how could they be friends?

She read the program from cover to cover: the notes on the pieces—the Debussy came after the interval, could she wait? She looked at the advertisements: Chateau Tanunda Brandy, Steinway, TAA and English Electric (pictures of overflowing fridges: 'Now two models to choose from!'). Advertisements for modern times, for prosperous times, an acquisitive life. But the things Nora longed for were not in these advertisements, it was not *things* she longed for.

She turned to Patrick, who was looking around him. People were coming in and finding their seats, waving to friends, reading the program. Patrick always looked around him with that determined attentiveness, well, he did every time they'd been out together. Tonight was the fourth time.

The orchestra members were taking their places. They began to tune their instruments. This scattering of sounds, the rising volume as eighty-odd separate instruments were being tuned and dozens of people took their places, was for Nora a delicious prelude to the experience that would follow. Out of this chaos of sounds there would be sublime order.

The tuning of instruments died away, the audience quietened. The concertmaster came out to the front of the orchestra and the leaders of the sections tuned with him, then he took his place. Everyone was quiet now; the audience sat as erect and attentive as the orchestra.

You didn't have to know much about music, Patrick reflected, to know who he was, the man everyone awaited. That was being top of your field: being known to the public, being known outside your own field. This was the man whose name all the newspapers knew, the man who earned more than the Prime Minister!

The conductor wrote letters to the editor, replying to his critics; social columns mentioned all his concerts. What had Patrick heard? That the conductor was bored stiff with Sydney society, preferred to be alone, or even . . . he'd heard something, what? Did the conductor keep a mistress? No, that was the broadcasting bloke. You had to take notice of these things, of everything you heard, you never knew when it might come in useful. Remember everything, Patrick instructed himself—an instruction he gave himself often: always take notice and remember. They had gossiped about the conductor at the paper, but at the time he hadn't yet met Nora and didn't know he'd ever be interested. That's right, it was the conductor's wife he'd heard about. She went to Europe to meet another man, and hadn't come back. Over a year ago. And the conductor had created a controversial

19

international competition for a new building for concerts. What was wrong with this one?

The orchestra rose, the audience applauded: Eduard von Kronen strode onto the podium, a tall authoritative man with a high, broad forehead, thinning hair, heavy-lidded eyes. He bowed to the house, a slight, elegant bow without any flourish. Then he turned to the orchestra. Then there was a still moment. Then he raised his arms. Then the first notes . . .

That still moment! Nora, when she took up her violin to practise, would think of that moment: a moment in which random, dispersed energies were drawn as if through a magic funnel, to be concentrated in the maestro.

That still moment. The woman in the back row was remembering the first time she had seen Eduard conduct. She had crept in tonight after all the audience was inside; her tickets were always kept at the door for her. She occasionally used them. She sat at the very back so as not to be stared at in her man's suit and leopard-skin shoes. She watched Eduard closely: he *was* the orchestra. At the beginning of each piece he became that stillness, and then raised his arms into stillness, the stillness that had shown her that he might teach her something.

Listen to that, thought June Henry. So clear, precise, pure. That orchestra is really sounding good now. And we all know why. They don't get away with anything now. Isn't it funny how it's men, it's usually men, who want it to be more emotional. A man likes a good tune and a bit of heart-stirring, she thought, and it's the women who appreciate the subtlety and purity of the sound. It was interesting.

The interesting part to Nigel Donne, music critic for the *Daily Mail*, was that the maestro was evidently bored and jaded. It was evident to him, at least. The other two critics might have their own views on that. Donne was sitting with his wife, at a discreet distance from his colleagues on the *Post* and the *Times*, though all the critics would get together at interval: a mutual protection society, they said.

For most of the audience, Donne thought, it might as well

20

be a machine out there, beating time. If it were a machine with a reputation for well-cut suits, lady-killing charm and European accolades, they'd think it was brilliant. The whole season had been conducted in a mechanical way. Was that going too far? No, say that, make a note. He'd always said von Kronen was too cold—there was no warmth in his interpretation, just as there was no lyricism in his music. Of course lyricism departed with the twelve-tone, and there were to be more of those infernal pieces tonight. Most of this twelve-tone stuff you wouldn't recognise as music at all, written by a crowd of phonies who couldn't write a tune if they tried—they couldn't recognise a tune. How many of these works in the new idiom were ever repeated? One performance and they were dead! Yes, that's the kind of thing he would say. The discerning reader would be guided to the inference that the credit 'first performance in Australia' was a more important consideration than any intrinsic worth the music had. They, the audience, were being used, used to add dubious credits to an orchestra's curriculum vitae and a conductor's reputation.

Dick Greene was making his own notes. He knew what they said about him. 'He doesn't know a crotchet, he can't write the key of G sharp minor,' they said. He was considered the ignoramus among music critics. He had had no musical training, that was true. But he liked to think that gave him some advantages. It enabled him to discuss music in a fresh, unprejudiced fashion. Dick Greene had his own review to think about. Although Sir Eduard was leaving the city tomorrow, for six months abroad, he would be sure to have the reviews sent on to him. The conductor was never indifferent to what was said about him. He did not take criticism lightly, however exalted his reputation.

Neville Henry came to the concert because his wife June bought the tickets, marked the dates on the calendar, and reminded him when they were to go. Of course, with his position at the Australian Broadcasting Commission he had to be seen to take an interest. He wouldn't say he minded. He often met visiting divas and soloists from overseas. Once there had been an extremely charming contralto. And when he was here, at the concert, he welcomed the chance to just sit and think. It was nice to drift away and have a bit of a think while you were sitting there, as long as you didn't nod off. June told him you were meant to 'follow', and not to drift away. He used to try to tell her how he liked music for the chance it gave him to think his own thoughts, but June would say you were meant to be thinking about the music. What could you think, he'd like to know, *about* music? You listened, there was nothing to *think*. He tried, as June had told him to, to think about the music, to follow it, but soon found he was drifting along on his own thoughts, as if the music were the current of a stream, his mind a raft bobbing along on it and his body lying passive on top.

During the interval Patrick read the program, especially the notes on the piece Nora was looking forward to, *Prélude à l'après-midi d'un faune*: 'It is like a beautiful sunset; it fades as one looks at it.'

When it began, Patrick again stole a sideways glance. That rapt, riveted look on Nora's face! And then he felt an awful tickle in his throat and, oh God, he was going to cough. He tried not to, he shut his mouth tight and swallowed hard but his mouth was so dry and his throat so inflamed that the swallowing irritated his throat more and he had to 'erkhh erkhh'. He tried to make it a little subdued cough, a little scarcely noticeable throat-clearing, but just as he did the music was barely whispering, there was the quietest sound, a little breeze on the water sound, and all around him they could hear him. Nora minutely stiffened, brought out of her entrancement, and minutely darted a cold glance in his direction, and minutely moved away from him.

Patrick is sitting there with his throat dry raspy itchy scratchy, screaming for a soothing cleansing cough, but he can't, he can't. The tears run from his eyes with the effort. Horror! he might look as if he is crying. Hey, that might go down well here, Nora might think he is a real sensitive bloke, artistic, all moved to tears by the gorgeous music—and she might forgive him. But nothing can stop this—a violent 'Urkkkkkhh urkhkh' that shakes itself all the more fiercely out of him as he tries to stop it short. He can't look at her, can't see her fury. Her body stiffens and leans away from him. Oh God, there go all his hopes, destroyed in the raucous dissonance of his unstoppable cough.

5
AT THE CROSS

'I don't know how you could live up there among all the criminals and drug addicts and Satanists.' I'd heard that quite a few times.

'It's not really like that,' I'd say, or I'd say, 'You get used to it.'

Kings Cross was my first home in Sydney. I'd come up from the country. My first job on the city paper, D-grade. Dream come true. Hit the big time. I needed a cheap room, and there were plenty of boarding houses round the Cross. I could walk to the paper from there, too.

The Cross had long had a racy reputation. Maybe I'd planned to live up there all along, maybe I'd dreamed of streets filled with gangsters and showgirls and beatniks. The reality took the place of the dreams and new dreams were created. I got to like it up there, at the Cross, and it was a long time before I moved out. I liked being around other people who didn't want to live in the suburbs, didn't want houses and gardens and kids and the P&C, didn't want to go to bed at the same time every day, the same time as everyone else in the street. I liked the streets that weren't all full of the same kind of people. It wasn't where I'd come from, that was its main attraction.

The Cross fancied itself as a place where things happened that sent out ripples forever. But it wasn't as wicked as people made out, nor as glamorous, nor as cosmopolitan. It was just a little district in a little city on the edge of nowhere.

There were mansions with huge gardens, and there were terrace houses with cheap bedsits. There were families who had been there since the colony was founded; there were rooms you could rent by the hour. All of Sydney's artists must have lived there at some time. It was the place for men with no fixed address;

it was the place for women who were escaping the kitchen sink; it was the place for juvenile delinquents to parade their pseudo-American clothes, while risking a charge of vagrancy at any time. Other languages besides English were heard in its streets and cafes. In the early mornings, drunken sailors would be rolling home while the Crossites, the old people who'd always lived there, went out for their milk and newspapers in their dressing-gowns and pyjamas, and sat on their verandahs telling the news to their neighbours.

People from the suburbs would come up to have a peek at the wicked part of Sydney. The Crossites called them 'tourists'. The Minerva cinema was always a good excuse, the tourists would see the latest film and then have a walk around, have a cup of tea somewhere. They'd stare and nudge, looking for artists and criminals and witches, then they went home and made it all up. What was there to see?

I'd sit for hours over one cup of coffee, listen to the piano player at the Globe, watch the people at the Himalaya, think about writing at the Cairo.

Separate from my life at the Cross was my life at the paper. I was learning a lot there. On the job, the only way. No degrees in journalism in those days. Did a lot of learning in the after-work 'sessions'.

The pubs closed at six o'clock. Men would rush into a pub after work, order a line-up of beers and down them as quickly as possible before closing time. This was supposed to keep men with their families and the streets free of crime. Did nothing of the sort, of course. You could always get a drink at any time, if you knew where to go.

The reporters would drink at a pub near Central and after six o'clock, when the front bar was being emptied and the doors were being closed, they would simply move into a back room. The cops would be paid off to leave the place alone and they'd been known to join the odd session themselves. The word 'corruption' was never uttered: this was the way things were and it was all accepted as part of the natural order of things.

I'd been around long enough and in some tacit way had proved myself, so I was being asked along. I went and I kept my mouth shut and my ears open—advice I've never forgotten—and tried to keep up with their drinking. All part of learning to be a good reporter. 'The silent type,' they'd kid me; they talked knowingly of the city and crudely of women, and I'd listen and then I would walk back home, saving the tram fare.

My head would be full of newspaper gossip, city gossip, and that restless feeling that makes young men imagine they are unique and that great things are in store. It was on one of those nights that I met Nora.

I wanted a girlfriend. I had visions of myself as an adult in the city and visions of myself as a man who knew about women. I thought of a fresh blonde teenager, perhaps still at school; I'd visit her and we'd go to the zoo, on picnics, for walks, she would look up to my superior age, experience and intellect. I thought of a dark older woman, worldly and experienced, who would initiate me into adult love, she would take me to her mansion, her husband would be away, there would be passion and tragedy. I looked at the prostitutes around the streets and jolly, fat old Meryl—she was over forty—who lived at my boarding house, and I thought about visiting a gay girl. I'd be her favourite, she'd ask me for nothing; I would wander and roam and succeed and see her rarely; she would follow my career and retire from her own, regretting only the loss of me. No, I don't know what I thought, and I didn't know what I wanted.

Then I met Nora and she dominated my visions of women: her exotic looks, her seriousness, her dignity.

I never knew any migrants before I met her. European migrants. Reffos, they were called. Refugees was too solemn a word. Wogs. Balts, bloody Balts. People used to speak about reffos as if they were not decent normal people.

And I'd never thought of young women dreaming not of rescue and security but of achievement. Nora's ambition was as much of a challenge as her foreignness. But it intrigued me, her history and her way of life and her desires did intrigue me. Maybe I had moments of regret for the fresh blonde I had never met: her passivity and simplicity. Maybe I missed the unknown older woman who would force me abruptly into jaded adulthood. It's always that way.

Nora and I started going out together, a walk around the streets, a coffee in one of the cafes. It was all new to me, walking round the streets for hours, talking with a girl, telling her everything I ever thought about. We were twenty years old. In those days that was young. I took her to see a film and she took me to a concert. I didn't know anything about music. I learnt a bit then, and it's made a difference ever since. She'd tell me what had been happening at the restaurant. I'd tell her things I'd hear about at the paper. At the time I thought the paper more important.

6
THE TWO CITIES

The Two Cities had a warm, welcoming light. Inside, it looked fearfully posh, with cloths on the tables and sparkling glasses. There was a group of people talking loudly. Some reffo language. I had stepped inside, and felt too awkward to just turn around and walk out.

'Table for one?'

'Yes,' I said.

At first I didn't take any notice of the waitress who showed me to my table, a small table against the far wall. She stood and waited while I read the menu—I remembered with relief that I'd got my pay that day—and I looked up at her. First sight. I don't know what you can feel about a person at first sight but when I saw her I wanted to stare and stare. Her hair and eyes were so dark. She seemed more *alive* than any girl I'd ever looked at. She looked right back at me.

'Are you ready to order?' she said. Later I realised that she still had a trace of an accent, though she'd lived in Australia since she was a kid.

'What would you recommend?'

'Continental or Australian?'

'Continental.' I intended to be as sophisticated as I could. 'Wiener schnitzel, gulyas, stuffed peppers . . .'

The most exotic thing I'd ever eaten was spaghetti, once.

'Have the schnitzel,' she said, and I was glad the ordering was over.

'To drink?' she asked. 'For wine,' she reminded me, 'you must have ordered before six p.m.'

'Barbaric,' I said, having studied some editorials on the subject.

28

Her eyebrows shot up. 'We agree,' she said and really looked at me.

When she came back with the wiener schnitzel she put a full glass down as well. I didn't realise what it was, so I guess she went away disappointed at the lack of reaction.

I ate my strange solitary late dinner. The vegetables were cooked with extra flavourings, the meat was thin and white and covered in fried breadcrumbs. I'd never thought much about food before, but this I ate slowly, wonderingly.

There was a background hum of foreign voices and foreign music—someone playing a piano. I would never know what impulse made me walk into the Two Cities that night, a kind of place I'd usually think belonged to a further-off future. I guess I didn't want to wait too long for my future. I imagined I was starting to live the way I'd planned to: foreign situations, foreign possibilities. Here I was eating at a table for one in a European restaurant with cloths on the tables and musicians playing! I didn't notice that two large men in uniform had come in. Large, of course they were large. Burly. As I took a sip of my drink I looked up and saw them. They were talking with the proprietress, a blonde woman in her thirties—Nora's aunt Magda, as I would soon know well. At that moment I realised it was a sharp sour alcoholic drink in my glass: wine.

The cops went round to all the tables. If wine was being drunk, they looked for the name on the bottle, as if for proof it had been ordered before the legal time-limit. It could not be proved, of course, but they were only throwing their weight around, trying to intimidate Magda. I heard them say they were 'just looking around'.

One of the cops lurched over to me and lifted my glass and sniffed it. Nora was right behind him. 'This gentleman is our guest,' she said.

The cop turned and stared at her. 'That right?' he said. 'Isn't he lucky. You don't ask me to be your guest.' He looked at me. 'I've seen you,' he said.

'Patrick Morris, *Daily Mail*,' I said. 'I was in with Col O'Brien the other day. Police rounds.'

29

'A mate of Col's?' the cop said. He looked at me for a practised long moment—they get their timing right, these cops. 'Good on ya,' he said. And he joined the other one, and left.

Nora was still standing near me. 'Thank you, Patrick Morris,' she said. Not overly grateful, not sarcastic either.

'Thank *you*,' I said. 'Nice wine. Good food.' She gave me a smile that sent my insides spinning. I don't know how I finished my meal.

She came back to see if I wanted more and I found out that it was her aunt's restaurant and that Nora was a student as well as a waitress and that they'd had a few problems with the cops ever since they'd opened the Two Cities.

She came back with my bill and told me her name. 'Nora Ujhazy,' she said, as if daring me to say it right. I did—and I couldn't even pronounce *merci beaucoup*.

She came back with my change and said we might run into each other. And I made sure we did.

7

AFTER THE CONCERT

After the first symphony concert I had ever been to, we walked up William Street to the Cross.

'Kronen,' I said. 'This might sound dumb, but it looks like he's got the easiest job of all. The others all have to play an instrument. He's up there just keeping time.'

Nora said, 'They only play one instrument. He plays the orchestra!'

I found it hard to understand. If a musical score gave you the notes, the tempo, even the manner, how could one conductor make the same piece sound so different from the way another did? Was it the way he kept time, never losing the beat? Was it his personality, making the players feel confident? Was it like being the coach of the cricket team?

'Yes,' said Nora. 'All those things. And things you don't see. Rehearsals. Forty instruments playing and he can hear *one* that is off-key. Style. Spanish music. They've never been to Spain. But he can express, show, make them see what a Spanish style is. Knowledge. He knows *so much* about music, especially modern music. Being modern, not stuck in the past.'

'Interpretation?' I wondered.

'Interpretation. One piece of music can be played quite a few different ways. I'll show you one day.'

'Actors speaking lines. Or interpreting a poem,' I offered, looking for analogies so I could understand.

'Eduard von Kronen,' she said, 'is . . .'

'Your mentor, your ideal, your inspiration?' I suggested.

'Absolutely.'

We had reached the Himalaya. It was a dark basement cafe that stayed open very late, one of the famous Cross hangouts.

I'd been there before, late at night, seen the flamboyant theatre folk, glossy-haired models and strange myopic artists. Men in black sweaters and girls in black sweaters stared with beatnik devotion into their black coffee. Nora hadn't been there before but I knew she would like it.

We found a seat, and Nora looked around and stared at the walls. They were covered with paintings; paintings of naked creatures with human faces in chilling grimaces; half-human bodies with hoofs, horns, animal ears and tails, sometimes three-eyed, holding thunderbolts or pointing ominously at the distance; they were intertwined with snakes, cats, bats, or strange reptilian creatures, watched over by pale sphinx-like faces with long feline eyes, faces worked into the paintings' backgrounds, sometimes barely discernible among the busy swirls of undulating line. As she stared at them, Nora half-rose in her seat as if in a sudden panic, then sat again. All the walls were covered in these paintings—behind us, opposite us, to either side. Among the fountains and clouds of line and colour lay spheres, pentacles and the six-pointed star, flames of fire, smoke, candles, many-petalled lotuses, towers and turrets, mandalas. It was the dreams and deliriums of all the symbolists clashed and shattered, their scattered components caught up in a maelstrom of febrile visions.

Nora said nothing.

'I take it you don't like them?' I said.

She shook her head uncertainly. 'They're strange,' she commented, inadequately and somewhat guardedly. Our coffee arrived. I put a lot of sugar in mine, always have.

'Eveleen Warden did these,' I explained. I'd already had a very long look at these paintings. They were strange, all right, stranger than anything I'd ever imagined, and I'd thought I had a good imagination.

Nora knew who she was, everyone did. Evvi had even been into the Two Cities. 'She came in with a friend, another woman who looked a bit like her,' Nora told me. 'They ordered lots of food, more than they could eat, dessert, everything. They wanted the leftovers wrapped to take home. The bill came—they had no money! They didn't seem worried, just looked around. At that moment, someone they knew walked in, and he paid for them.'

I'd already heard a few stories about Eveleen Warden.

'And she said,' Nora continued, ' "Oh there you are!" She said "I conjured you up." Just as if she knew someone would come along and pay.'

'She's supposed to be a witch.'

Nora just smiled and shook her head, not telling me what she really thought.

'I'd like to interview her,' I said.

'What would you ask her?'

I didn't know. 'Where her ideas come from.'

Nora's eyes kept flickering over the paintings. We had already had a discussion about nudity and art, and the beauty of the human body. I got the impression that Europe was covered with beautiful statues of naked bodies and that there it was considered comical to be either offended or stimulated by them. We had agreed that prudery was anti-art and we were pro-art, absolutely. I wasn't sure if being pro-art allowed you to feel secretly stimulated by the sight of Evvi's naked writhing forms, those cat-eyed round-bellied women entwined with serpents.

It was a warm night. Nora and I took our usual walk, down Macleay Street and Wylde Street. We found a place where we could sit and look at the moonlight on the water between us and Mrs Macquarie's Chair.

We'd seen a bit of each other by now. I'd held her hand, then I'd put my arm around her, then one night kissed her. We were young, those days were different, you took your time. In those days nice girls weren't supposed to 'go all the way', that's how they put it, but Nora and I believed that two people who loved each other *should* express it to the fullest, to hell with bourgeois moralism. I don't know what I'd have said if anyone asked me where I got my ideas from.

That night, our kisses grew longer and deeper, she let me touch more and more of her soft warm body, but not inside her clothes, not yet. That night she promised she would. Let me feel

33

inside. Soon. It was soon enough for me. I mean, it *wasn't* soon enough for me. But I was intoxicated by her promises and by my infatuation with my own life, and all that was pretty satisfying in itself.

After I'd left Nora at her place I began walking home. It was around midnight and still a mild night. Spring. Even in the city it was spring, though there were fewer signs: only the warmer nights and the new leaves appearing on the plane trees. Back home, lambs were growing, and it was time to crutch the sheep again. If I never saw another shit-caked sheep's arse it would be too soon for me.

Home, where the family was. No, that used to be home. Home now was was my cramped rented room with its single bed, the table in the corner, the few things I owned: some clothes, some books, the old family clock my mother had given me.

I walked past the Hasty Tasty at the top of William Street, then turned and went inside and ordered a hamburger, because now I could eat whenever I felt like it. I lived in the city now. I lived in Kings Cross, I worked on a newspaper and one day I would be a senior reporter, a journalist. I would interview the Prime Minister, I would expose criminals. There would be another war and I would go to the front line and send my dispatches. I would grow into a well-travelled, worldly man. I would leave the newspaper and write a book. About what? It didn't matter. I would have a lot of experience by then. People would wish they knew what I knew. They would be bloody amazed at the things I could tell, the way I could tell it.

I finished my hamburger and wandered down Bayswater Road, away from the Cross, no longer headed home. I felt exultant and disturbed. I *knew* things about myself. I felt myself grow harder, stronger, more adult. I felt the world open out and show me a glimpse of its vastness. I felt terrified by my smallness. I felt I could grow huge and conquer it all. I felt very alone. Did anyone else ever feel this? If they spoke about it what did they say? I wanted to know everything.

I reached Rushcutters Bay Park. I walked to the water's edge.

The water was dark opal, lit with the reflections of stars. I turned and leaned on the stone wall, and saw how the trunks of the trees glowed. I could see everything but things had no colour in the dark. Darkness was another world, the shadow of the world. Nora would hold me tight and we would gaze at the moonlight on the trees and kiss and *not stop*. I walked over to a smooth-barked tree and pulled out the penknife I always carried. I cut a heart into the tree. I traced over the shape again, to cut it deeper. Why was I doing this? Now what? Our initials? Only her name? N: I would write only N. I began to carve: a downward slash enclosed by a heart. Then I looked up.

It was her! That woman, the witch, Eveleen Warden, in her strange clothes. The one who had painted those weird paintings and been arrested for obscenity and who frequently gave cheek to the cops. She drifted towards me, she had seen me, she was watching me with her black feline eyes. I watched her approach, my hands still holding the knife to the heart on the tree.

She spoke. 'I hope you asked the spirit of this tree for its blessing before marking its physical form?'

I dropped my hand. 'No, I didn't think of that.'

'When I cast spells,' she said, 'I know what I am doing, and my spells are effective. Do you have a cigarette?'

I flipped the blade back into its case and put it back into my pocket, took out my cigarettes and matches. In the semi-dark I saw that her velvet cloak was a wine-red colour. She wore trousers and sandals. A leopard-skin scarf was tied round her head. Her voice was pleasant, soft and educated.

She drew the smoke right into her lungs, and held onto the packet of cigarettes.

She looked at the tree, at the heart I had carved there. 'Love magic,' she said. 'Love, money, power, revenge. People want me to give them spells, simple spells, easy to use potions, and they don't understand what they want.'

I didn't know what to say. I didn't know what she was talking about but she didn't sound mad or bad to me. She had a nice voice and she sounded quite sane and rather smart.

She held out my packet of cigarettes. I took one out and lit it, took another out and put it in my pocket, and handed the packet back to her. She took it and gazed round the park. Then she turned and strolled away.

8

THE WITCH OF THE CROSS

Mick's Milk Bar, it was called. After me. My own business. Nothing
fancy. A cafe type of place, a few booths down the side to sit
at. I owned it and worked in it; served toasted sangers, meat
pies, hamburgers. Milk shakes, tea. Old-fashioned Aussie tucker.
There were a lot of new joints around. Yankee-style joints, or
the New Australians. I never changed, though. Kept the place
on till about 1960. Newsagent there now or some bloody thing.
I'd get mainly local people, regulars, who'd have the same thing
every day, and you'd get to know them pretty well.

Oh, yeah, we all knew her. All kinds of people came to look
for her place—they'd want to say they'd seen a real witch. Witch!
She used to be known as the girl who drew pictures while she
was in a trance, then the 'witch' business started. The Crossites
reckoned the papers started it—suddenly they'd be reading about
'black masses', 'orgies' and 'Satanism'. We'd have a bit of a laugh.
'Hey Evv,' some of us would call out, 'having a black mass
tonight?' Evvi would laugh it off mostly; sometimes she would
give them a bit of a lecture if they would listen. She didn't believe
in the Christian mass, she'd say, so why would she have a black
mass, she'd say, and so on. She'd go on about it but no one
took much notice. Live and let live.

Everyone up here at the Cross knew Eveleen—her and that
skinny boy, Terry the Poet, who was often with her. Up the Cross
they used to say, 'What an imagination, eh?' They all knew about
her trances. They knew she could make her mind a vast empty
plain and all the spooks and demons would come galloping in
and rushing around and she would draw them. They knew she
really believed in gods and symbols and spirits: they'd rush in
too, if you wanted them to.

37

All the creatures she drew looked a bit like Eveleen herself, with those slanty cat's eyes. Evv would shave off her eyebrows and draw high, pointy ones. She'd wear a little fringe and short hair that showed her pointy ears. She would say her pointy ears were a mark of being a witch; that, and some other features she claimed to have. She told the magazines she had the witch's marks: mounds on her feet, some kind of strange sinew from armpit to waist, certain spots. Some people said she only made it all up. Wouldn't like to say, myself.

First it was no, no don't call me a witch, then suddenly it was yes, I am a witch. No one listened when she tried to tell them the truth about witches and demons, that it'd all been made up by the Christians, or whatever. But if she said 'all right, have it your way, I'm a witch', and blacked out her teeth just for fun—then she was treated a bit more seriously, and was used to frighten children.

People who didn't live in the Cross, or who didn't really know her, used to think she was really creepy. Out at Bondi, mothers told their naughty kids to 'behave, or the witch'll get you! Eveleen Warden will get you!'.

You had to know when Evvi was having you on. She could tell you something so seriously, and she'd just be pulling your leg. Then another time she'd be furious if you didn't believe her. Maybe she took a few too many pills.

She hadn't been taken too seriously as an artist, but she could always get attention. You wouldn't know if Eveleen had ever been much of an artist. She did have talent, but then she became more of a personality, a minor celebrity, someone to be written about and talked about.

Evvi had been known round the Cross since her art school days. She'd always been flamboyant-looking—you'd have to notice her. She was a nice person, though. I never used to mind her. If she came in for some tea and couldn't pay I'd say, 'Any old time'll do.' She said she'd give me a painting but I declined. She said she'd give me some protection thing to wear but I said, 'Keep it, love, I can look after myself'. Evv'd be decent to you if you respected her, but she could get bloody vicious otherwise.

The cops hated her. She'd give them terrible cheek. If a couple of detectives were coming towards her, she'd say, loudly, 'Well look at the big dicks. Are you cleaning the Cross of all its vice?' Someone in the street would laugh, but the cops never thought it was a bit funny. They hated her, the cops, and she got hauled in that time.

She and that boy had something going. It wasn't like they were having a big romance, but he was around her all the time. He went round the twist later on, poor coot, and got put in the bin. Think he went inside a few times all in all.

She was a fair bit older than him, and he was a bit fey, tall and skinny and not all there. He wrote poetry, had some of it printed in some little magazine when he was only thirteen! He came from a top family too, like she did. Her father was a Navy captain and his father was a top journalist; bloody communist they reckon, another reason they were so hated by the Ds. Poofters, commos, weirdos—cops always hated them. Some of them still do.

You'd hear Evvi and Terry were into devil worship. Sheer nonsense, of course. Evvi had a picture of a demon painted over her fireplace. A lot of people had seen it: everyone got down to Evv's place some time or other. What was all the fuss about? It was just a filthy place with strange mess everywhere. But a lot of people would go there and think: this is the life, bohemians and witches! And they'd have a little think about what might go on in there after they'd left: never knew what a good imagination they had till they thought of all the wicked things other people must be getting up to.

Well, some funny things did go on, I heard, but it wasn't for the tourists. Evv would pick some young fellas to go down there, and the others'd pay to get in. The word would go round that she was having one of her nights. She and Terry the Poet, they'd get everyone round in a circle and they'd be dressed up and go on with a whole lot of bloody rigmarole, chanting and wailing, and then she'd pick the blokes in turn and they'd get it off with her, get their cocks sucked too, that was the big thing in those days; get to stick it in Terry too, if they wanted. I never went myself, I was shy in those days.

Anyway, there was that picture on the wall and everyone would swear it was the devil, with its horns and hoofs and tail, but no, says Evvi, this was Pan, and getting Pan confused with the devil was the biggest problem most people had, according to Evvi. The devil was made up by the Christians and Pan was a nature god from the olden days. See, I had a fair few talks with her but I don't remember half the stuff she used to go on about, made no sense to me.

People from all over came to look for Eveleen Warden's place; she'd get quite a few rich people and society people down there. After the book came out, and after the raid on her paintings, she'd become quite famous in this town, and a lot of people just wanted to be able to say they'd met her. There'd even be men who'd have a go, try to get her to come across; they wanted to say they'd done it with a witch. They could have too, if they'd had the right connections.

Some of them wanted to buy her paintings. A lot of them asked for 'Lucifer', that's what they used to call the one on her wall.

'You can't have that one,' she'd say, 'but I'll paint you one just like that.' Then she'd touch them for a little advance to get her started and they'd be so excited they'd pay up. So she'd go out and buy some bread and some paints.

The client would come round to see how she was going. 'I'll need a bit more,' she'd say, having figured this one as a soft touch. 'I need my dexies to keep going, without my dexies I can't stay up all night and get your painting done for you.'

So the client gave her more money, and on it went. Finally the painting would be done, and he'd paid its worth several times over. And then what could he do with it? He'd got all carried away but now he had a painting he couldn't show anyone. So it got rolled up and put in the back of a cupboard to be found by the wife when she was having a big clean-up and then it got burnt with all the rubbish.

9
MIGRATIONS—EDUARD

Eduard von Kronen knew few things about Sydney when he was first invited to visit Australia. He knew that it was a lovely and remote city, founded by the English. He knew that there they were looking for a conductor.

Before he accepted the invitation, he found out a little more. The Australian Broadcasting Commission was the government-owned and controlled national broadcaster, and it was about to form a new full-time orchestra. And they wanted a world-class conductor to lead it. The war was over and there was an opportunity to enter the new age. They wanted to be thought of as a nation, not a colony.

It's said that conductors can be divided into two kinds: orchestra-builders and guest conductors. Eduard von Kronen had proved himself an excellent builder of orchestras, as his Australian hosts knew. He had already turned one provincial little American band into an orchestra that now commanded worldwide respect.

He could do the same here! they said in Australia. He could do a lot, he could help make this raw, new country a part of the world (the British, European, American world). Would he want to? The Australians invited him on a tour, let him know what they were looking for, and laid their bets. It was seven to three against, then.

The Australian Broadcasting Commission prided itself in impeccability in the matter of correct English. Their announcers spoke with BBC accents and wore evening dress to read the news. Von Kronen, although from an old Dutch family—generations of acclaimed musicians—was a first-generation Englishman, and very English indeed. In spite of having spent the last fifteen years in America, Eduard's pronunciation was

41

also impeccable. This they could prove for themselves when he got here. It was reported with satisfaction that he pronounced 'schedule' the way an Englishman does. He was, for their purposes, an Englishman; and thus, as England defined the desirable and England was Home, he was best qualified to lead the Australians to world culture.

The directors of the Australian Broadcasting Commission made sure that Eduard's first visit was pleasant. They took him out on a ferry to Manly Beach. From the middle of the bright blue waters they looked back at the hills of Sydney that led down to the many bays and coves that fringed its beguiling harbour. If Faust were offered his temptations again, he would be taken not to a mountain top but to the middle of Sydney Harbour. Eduard's observations were gratifying. Here was a lovely unspoiled place, he remarked, here was a country of the future. Here, one could do as well as in America. This, now, was the New World! At Manly they ate fresh prawns in the sunshine by the pine trees. He willingly ate them with his fingers. The only way to do it, he said, and his hosts laughed appreciatively.

Australia was taking its first confident steps into a decade of advancement and prosperity. So far from the rest of the world (*the world*: Britain, Europe, the United States), this pretty city looked endearingly old-fashioned to the visitor from America. It was as if the war had not touched it. Australian soldiers had sailed abroad to have their war and when the country's own shores were threatened it was on the other side of the vast continent, several deserts and thousands of miles away. Many Sydneysiders' memory of the war was one of high-wired spendthrift Americans—one long party. It was a safe, optimistic city that the conductor saw. (Later, he would have to agree that it was also a country ripe for fascism. The complacency of the place was concomitant with a xenophobic small-town moralism.)

Eduard's reticent speculations were encouraged. Yes, the Australians agreed, Sydney could combine the best of European and American cities: its English origins (colonial architecture— some charming examples along Macquarie Street were pointed out) and its new world freshness. He knew he would be asked to extend his visit indefinitely.

They let him look around to consider. He considered. Here was a challenge. There were new fields to conquer. Here was a pleasant way of life. Here he would be a very important person in a very small society. There was a leading part in the future. There was a fantastic challenge.

First he faced his immediate test: the tour. Eduard von Kronen worked with the newly formed orchestra, which included musicians of considerable experience and others who had never played in an orchestra before. In the little time available he gave them a sense of unity. They responded to his authority, his patience, his experience.

The orchestra's members were forced to play better than they knew how, better than they dreamed they could. They even performed Stravinsky's *The Rite of Spring* and entered the modern age. (Only a few people walked out.)

And they played an unsettling piece called *The Dreaming* and gave birth to an astonishing notion: the Australian Composer. Von Kronen had insisted on finding and playing an indigenous composition on this tour and they found one for him. *The Dreaming*, played on European instruments and with European melodies, captured the vastness and eerie timelessness of the country's distant interior, and the ancient songs of its native people. It took a while for the implications to sink in, and eventually people began asking new questions. Was there a possibility of a distinctly Australian musical idiom? Could the music of the Aborigines be another source for this new Australian music? A long way from being answered, the questions themselves created a still imperceptible but long-resounding change.

Before von Kronen left the proposal was made. Would he regard the place as impossibly faraway, too parochial, too colonial? But the ones who bet on his accepting the offer won. The odds were seven to three on by this time.

So that they could afford him, Eduard was to be given a position as head of the School of Music as well as Principal

Conductor of the Sydney Symphony Orchestra. The combined salaries and allowances were by Australian standards astronomical. 'More than the Prime Minister!' the papers gasped. So that they could entice him, he was offered a contract whose terms provided the humming and buzzing of gossip and more stories for the papers. 'He can do what he likes!' they summed up.

He was to be paid an extra fee for concerts conducted outside the subscription series. He'd receive a first-class airline ticket for himself and his family every year so he could take conducting engagements throughout the world. He'd have full control over the orchestra: the right to fire, hire, decide on the programs.

No one had had these rights before, and it would be a long time before a conductor was offered them again. No, not because von Kronen was a tough negotiator, he wasn't. He seemed diffident and vague about money. He was offered these terms, and he accepted them.

In 1949 he arrived back in Australia to take up his positions. He sailed into Sydney Harbour with his new wife and his child, and they were photographed leaning over the rails of the ship's deck, waving to the pressmen, the radiomen, the wives.

Everyone begged him for a statement, and he had one ready. 'I shall make,' he said, 'the Sydney Symphony Orchestra one of the six best in the world.'

The world? Australia? Music? Best? In the world!

10
MIGRATIONS—EVELEEN

The year after Eduard arrived Eveleen Warden had still not heard of him. She was having her own big year. There was an exhibition of her paintings in Melbourne.

At last, she thought, as she hitched the long way south with Terry, at last, at last. At last, she would receive recognition of her talent as an artist and recognition of her ability as an occultist.

As it turned out, she was recognised only as a painter of dirty pictures.

In Sydney the police had already taken paintings of hers from the walls of a popular late-night artists' haunt. In Sydney, though, they were philistines, ignorant, the police force dominated by the Catholics. In Melbourne, she was told, it wouldn't be like that; Melbourne was more European, the people more sophisticated.

In Melbourne the pictures had been hung in a hall at the university. And in Melbourne too police raided the exhibition and seized the paintings, and Eveleen was charged with having exhibited obscene pictures. Said one of the papers:

> She out-Lindsays Norman Lindsay at voluptuous compositions—but she lacks Norman's skill . . .
> She's probably the only artist whose drawings make other artists' hair stand on end . . .
> She is not represented in the National Gallery.

Said Eveleen acerbically to the press: 'I am intrigued to learn that the cultural standards of the Victorian police are greater than that of Professor Munro who opened the exhibition. Or of anyone in Adelaide, where the pictures were exhibited without incident.'

Eventually the charge was overturned, but still the exhibition didn't make her any money, as all the students from the university used to sneak in without paying to see the 'rude pictures', and hardly anyone else came.

She considered her career so far. She had still been at school when a small magazine had published some of her drawings and precocious stories. Her stories were childish, gruesome little fantasies of horror. In one, possessing spirits forced a sculptor to create a hideous monster that came alive and devoured him; in another, high-spirited schoolgirls persuaded their chaperone to enter a tiger's cage at the zoo; the chaperone was horribly mauled and then torn to pieces.

The editors didn't want any more stories from her, but she was given a few assignments to illustrate other stories. Her drawings, full of oblique lines, grotesque beasts and obscure meanings, were distinctive, if unsettling. The job didn't last, she never came up with any funny gags for her pictures.

She had left art school before bothering to complete the course and gain a diploma. She never managed to earn much of a living. She tried, though. She heard of the pavement artists in Paris and went down to Rowe Street with her chalks and drew on the footpath of the narrow pedestrian street, and people would throw pennies at her, some of them. Most of them just looked and walked on, or called out rude comments. When someone threw a penny from an upstairs office window, and it only just missed her head, she knew she wasn't meant to be a pavement artist any more.

None of the jobs lasted long: delivering messages on a bicycle, serving in a cafe, and modelling for Life Drawing classes at East Sydney Art School (where once she had gone to classes) or for groups of artists who wanted the practice. She knew they usually preferred models with more meat on their bones, more curves and folds to their flesh, but then she was very good at holding poses for a long time; she liked doing that, setting challenges for herself, seeing how long she could go without moving, so she got the work.

46

She had even been married—a comradely marriage—for a while, before the war. They travelled down to Melbourne and up to Queensland together, hitching rides on steamtrains—'jumping the rattler' it was called. She saw most of the east coast of Australia this way, although nothing about it made a lasting impression and she never remarked on the beauties of the countryside she saw.

Evvi was not interested in landscape, or portraits, or even abstract expressionism. Her landscapes, her subjects, were all in her mind. She conjured up spirit-infested trances and hardly saw the hills, plains and trees out of the window of the chugging goods train. While she roved the country, in the only prolonged trip away from the city she ever took, she was planning her further studies. She believed in a Nature religion but did not care much for Nature. Though she made an occasional sketch of the vast expanses of countryside or the little towns they passed through, she mostly drew intersecting circles and the heads of women all slants and angles, and bodies of strange creatures, and shapes of ancient archetypal symbols.

Sometimes they stayed in the towns and, while her husband collected money, Eveleen would hypnotise a local lass. The townspeople bet that the strange woman from the Big Smoke could never make young Brenda or Mavis or Alice, whom they all knew well, utter strange words and incantations, or take off their cardigan and unbutton their blouse. Eveleen and her husband often won, and always left the town immediately.

Eveleen had been glad to get back to the city; she was made for the city for all her paganism. She didn't have too much in common with her husband, who got sick of spirits and ghosts and hocus-pocus and went off to war, which didn't impress her at all. So they didn't see much of each other after that.

The public knew about her; she had been written about in the papers and even interviewed about her trances and the esoteric influences she cultivated. This public attention aroused in her more contempt than satisfaction. It never represented her correctly. No one really appreciated her unique visions.

47

In private she was continuing her studies of the occult and ceremonial magic, experimenting with hypnosis, painting with a creative rush that produced all the images and themes she would use for the rest of her life.

She began to create the paintings that would be remembered, and while she longed for a great teacher and mentor, she found a young student and acolyte: a thin, young man, who wrote poetry, wore his hair long, and spoke intensely, in a shy whisper, of the symbols in his dreams. Terry the Poet became her devoted companion. He admired her passionately, and fetched and carried for her, and wanted nothing more than to serve her, and create works with her. As she moved from trances and simple rituals to more elaborate magical ceremonies, Terry joined with her, and allowed odd entities to be channelled through him.

Sexually he was extremely submissive, and became passive and feminine, and she scourged him and took him like a man would, using phallic objects; at other times she enjoyed his gentle caresses, his scratches on her back. Eveleen was reading Aleister Crowley's channelled book, *The Book of the Law*, and understood more than did nearly all of its uninitiated readers the messages about the power derived from ceremonial sexual experimentation.

Like many before her and many more after her, Eveleen thought that if a book were dictated from beyond this plane, it was truer than anything that was written in the normal way. She never questioned that 'beyond' held all knowledge and truth, and that anything that came from there had to be extremely valuable. Her readings on the Qabbala told her about the Tree and the ten planes, and, as far as she was concerned, to be in the everyday life of this earth was to be on the lowest plane of existence, and anything elsewhere was higher and better. If Crowley had written his book in a frenzy of supernatural possession, it was a great book and she would follow it. She could do it, too. Her own powers of concentration were supernatural by now.

Her rituals increasingly used sexual imagery and sexual practice and Terry the Poet was a frequent partner. Other people were partners too, from time to time, but those others mainly just wanted to get a root any way they could; here was a chance to put it up weird Evvi and to buggerise Terry, and if she made them sit through some bloody bell book and candle mumbo-jumbo to do it, well, good luck to her.

Some of the cafes around the place put her paintings on their walls, and that led to the trouble with the cops, who'd be tipped off by someone and would seize some of the pictures or close the place down or just take the check-up call as an opportunity to either bring a few people in for questioning or to rough-up a few of the juvenile delinquents.

She thought it would be different in Melbourne but it was more of the same. All these raids were nothing but a nuisance; the publicity was quite the wrong sort and did nothing to help sell her paintings or get her the recognition she deserved. But she did receive some recognition—as a possible psychological specimen, a subject for a case report . . .

A psychologist from the university where her troublesome paintings hung asked her to undergo some tests and a few sessions of analysis. What did he want? Did he think she had an interesting mind that he wanted to study? Did he hope to find a subject for a paper that might win him professional esteem: a woman who received visions in a trance and created powerful pictures, scandal and court cases? Maybe she would speak in tongues, or reveal new knowledge about the mind.

He asked her to lie on a couch, in the manner of psychoanalysis. She answered questions about her mother, father, siblings, school, early memories and then, in more detail, her sexual history. She had begun at the age of twelve with a boy her own age. It was painful and she did not try again. She made a second start at seventeen. She was very active, sexually, in her early twenties. 'First period: excessive but normal heterosexual relationships,' he wrote. Then she went through periods of preferring sex with male homosexuals, and female homosexuals, always taking the dominant role. She liked sado-masochistic sex; she liked being tied to a pole and beaten, she told him, and fucked so that her back was forced hard against the pole, hurting her. She liked beating men too, '. . . with a strap,' he wrote, 'and then having S.I.'.

'Sex, creation, magic, the imaginative fire,' she began. 'What I have always . . .' But the psychologist believed that the psyche was a matter of measurable components, and wanted only the facts, as he called them.

'And now,' said the psychologist, producing the Rorschach-Benn tests. She was to tell him what she saw in the ink blots.

'Oh, like using tarot cards, or tea-leaves,' she told him. 'They too were used as a symbolic focus . . .'

He dismissed this preposterous proposition. 'Psychologists are not witches,' he said with a thin smile, and handed her each card with the same question: 'Look at this card and tell me . . .'

She saw animals, and altars, an Egyptian mummy, ceremonial masks, winged masks, death masks, Rasputin, the Fall of the House of Usher, prehistoric creatures in battle . . .

'The amount of variety and fantasy is clearly not as great as the subject thinks it is,' the psychologist wrote in his report. '. . . Straining for originality . . . emotional rigidity . . . high degree of introversiveness . . . The subject is malingering in the direction of schizophrenia; she is trying to be odd and peculiar and to give way to unconscious fantasies . . . In attempting to label this subject, the closest approximation would be to say that she is a highly imaginative hysteric, who is endeavouring to cope with her anxieties by a process of working through them in fantasy, and an identification with a socially deviant and somewhat schizophrenic role.'

So Eveleen did not find her Jung and the psychologist did not find the great subject whose case could be published to make his name.

She went back to Sydney and made the decision: she would not take any more silly jobs. She would earn a living from her painting and her occult art.

'There goes the witch,' people would say. 'See her? That's the Witch of Kings Cross.'

11
MIGRATIONS—NORA

Nora put on a new pleated tunic and black stockings, filled her new Globite schoolcase with new notebooks and began high school.

A year earlier, she and her aunt Magda had moved to Sydney. Magda took her to the local primary school. The Central Office had decreed that Nora should be put in fourth class, with much younger children. The teacher realised this was because she was a poor little reffo who didn't speak English. The teacher seemed to think of this as an affliction closely allied to imbecility, and spoke to her in a slow, condescending way as if she were dimwitted.

One day Nora said, 'You don't have to speak to me that way. I understand everything you say.' Some children snickered and the furious teacher sent her out of the room for being cheeky. Nora dutifully reported to the Head.

It was lucky for Nora that the Head, Miss Glass, listened to her, and learnt that the child spoke English rather well—better, if the truth be known, than some of the local riff-raff—and she moved Nora into class 5A. A few weeks later Nora was sent out of the classroom for reading books under the desk during lessons, and reported again to the Head for punishment. Miss Glass found out that Nora was bored, that she had already learnt everything the class knew, or would be allowed to know that year. The Head knew the child lived with her aunt, and called the aunt in.

Miss Glass had travelled Home and to The Continent before the war, and so was less surprised than the other teachers when Magda came to the school. They all expected a broad, squat, peasant woman in a long black dress and head-scarf, and Magda was an elegant woman in a Chanel suit that never dated, and her English was perfectly distinct and educated, intelligible, in spite of a marked accent, which in fact was rather charming. Magda was more like the film image of the infinitely sophisticated Frenchwoman than the thick, comically screeching fishwife of their Balt jokes. Magda confirmed that Nora had already received a great deal of schooling, in spite of the disruptions to her life; she had begun at an international school in Rome, and on the ship and at the D.P. camp she had had many private tutors, including herself, and friends of hers: a couple, a professor and a writer. Nora loved to study, Magda explained, and was used to rapid progress. She was glad to have this conference, as she was afraid that Nora would be, how could she say? Please understand that she respected Australian schools very much, but here, where things were rather easier, the drive to excel was not valued, and the idea of equality was of course a wonderful thing, she, Magda, thought it was a very good idea, very interesting, this Australian idea that everyone was equal, for so they were, but Nora came home upset when the other children did not like her to know the answers and finish her exercises and read extra books, and apparently the teacher had once called little Nora 'Miss Smartypants' and so the children said it all the time now, and it made her cry. It would be a shame, a crime, if this child's love of books and knowledge were stifled. Now, she had an idea: Nora was old enough to go into sixth class, and of course she understood that she had not completed the preceding years, but she, Magda, she herself would supervise and make sure Nora caught up . . .

'Yes,' said Miss Glass, 'yes, how good, how kind, if only the other parents would take the time, take an interest.'

'Blab blab blab, you should have heard her,' reported 5A's teacher in the staffroom. ' "I wanna my kidda to learna da more-a," ' she mocked ineptly. 'Glasshouse had to say yes to shut her up. Crikey, they're pushy, foreigners. Our own kids wouldn't be allowed . . .'

So in the middle of that year Nora was placed in sixth class. She could never be popular at this school, or even liked, and she could not be accepted. All she could do was catch up, and recite her times-tables, and practise her running writing, and learn about Captain Cook and the governors, and paste cut-out pictures into her project books. At the end of the year she won a place at Sydney High School, which was selective, and a Commonwealth Bursary to help with her expenses.

'What do you remember, Noraska?' Magda asked her sometimes. 'Do you remember Budapest? Do you remember Rome? Do you remember the ship, and the Törleys who loved you so? Do you remember your father? Do you remember Mamika, darling? Does it make you sad to think of her?'

'I don't remember,' said Nora. 'Tell me and I'll remember.'

Nora's memories started with the primary school at Kings Cross where she had gone to three different classes in a year and where they hated her. She had amnesia about her life before that. She belonged to the exiles and their roots were laid in a mixture of memory and fable and forgetting. Her own memories were discovered in the stories Magda told her, or maybe those stories formed her memories.

On the long overnight train ride up to Sydney, Magda had wept. 'Because the seasons are upside down,' she'd explained as she sobbed quietly for a while. Here, the stars were topsy-turvy, everything was the wrong way round, it was the antipodes. Little Nora stroked her arms.

Then Magda had become cheerful and had said, 'Noraska, listen. Now we are in Australia we are like newborn babies—we have to learn again everything, how to talk, to find our way, everything. We shall look only forward, and speak only of the future. We shall speak in English, only English now.'

So Nora spoke to Magda in English, and Magda replied in Hungarian, a habit it took her a long time to break. 'I still *count* and *pray* in Hungarian,' she would say, and would continue to say for years.

They moved into a two-room flat at the Cross and Magda had to hand over all her funds for key money. There weren't many good flats around, and those that were around changed hands carefully. There were plenty of jobs and not enough workers, and at once Magda chose a job as a waitress, as it was closest to home. First she worked at one of the hamburger joints that had sprung up for the Americans during the war; and later at a cafe, where they served strong milky tea and scones, or a sandwich made from this spongy, thin white stuff that the Australians called bread.

Near their flat was a small Viennese cafe, which always had a queue of people waiting their turn to eat and move on. People who worked in clothes shops and cafes ate at the Viennese on their way home from work.

There was one baker in the whole of Sydney where you could buy real bread, and one butcher in the whole of Sydney where you could buy real meat, and Magda and others like her, all migrants, travelled once a week, if they could, to buy these things. At the Viennese cafe you could eat real food, but there was nowhere else, no nice, comfortable restaurant where you could meet friends, eat a good meal and linger and talk and drink.

Magda made a decent living and began to wonder if she could start her own business: a restaurant of her own. Her kind of people did not have their kind of place.

Magda's idea of *her kind of people* had a new meaning now. Class, race, religion—how could that matter any more? Some of the displaced people with her background held tight to the subtle discriminations they had been brought up to make, but Magda had lost nearly everything: parents, sister, lover, home and country. She had gained a niece who was now her daughter, and she had new ideas of her own. It was a new country and a new life. Her kind of people were all the dispossessed from Europe who needed to eat and drink and hear music and sit comfortably and talk to each other.

Hidden in her luggage—hidden and guarded and taken out behind locked doors and covered windows—were Magda's family jewels. She had learnt to recognise an opportunity, and when the time came she sold the jewels and bought the lease on a vacant restaurant on Darlinghurst Road. While the renovations

54

were being done, while the cops came and told her how much they wanted each week, while she shopped for tableware and collected recipes, she thought of a name for her restaurant.

Dickens's *A Tale of Two Cities* was an English book she had read with her governess. The title meant London and Paris, but her two cities were her birthplace, Budapest, and the city she might have to stay in forever now, Sydney. Budapest was itself a single city made of two separate cities on either side of the Danube. And this, too, this new life and new venture was 'the best of times and the worst of times'.

Nora believed the best and worst were left behind. For Nora, the past was the forbidden topic, the unanswered, unformed question whose answer held a key to herself. Her mind formed an image of an old European town: from the worn, cobbled street you see a row of old stone houses; it is crisply cool, there is an air of ancient tranquillity. From behind the lighted, curtained window of one of these solid, lovely buildings some music is heard, music as fleeting and scintillating as her dreams. What is it? Half asleep, Nora would think she knew: perhaps a string quartet, perhaps a trio with piano . . . shimmering music . . . but nothing she could capture in her conscious mind. That recurring snatch of a dream stayed with her, while her present reality was this brash strange land, its harsh light and harsh newness, people who looked at them unkindly and people who were kind.

Soon after she began high school her class was taken to a concert for schools in the Town Hall. She came home raving and never stopped talking about it. The orchestra! The conductor! The grand building and the pipe organs inside! The musicians, the music, the music.

Magda listened. Music and concerts were a memory of a misty past, the past that was shattered by those events that you had better not speak of now, and the long journey to Australia. Yes, Nora should learn to play. When Magda was growing up every young lady learnt to speak French, draw, and play the piano.

Even people who can't play music know which instrument they would play if they could. Do musicians choose their

55

instruments, or are they chosen by them? Nora began violin lessons, there was never any question about it. She learnt piano, too, later, but the violin was her instrument.

First she was taught to hold it like a banjo, and strum its strings, and then she could put it up on her shoulder, under her chin. She held it correctly at once, knowing how it felt just right. She did not need to be made to practise, though Magda had promised to force her if necessary. And she knew from the start it would be her career, she never considered anything else.

Other girls at high school lived with mum and dad in a house with a yard and ate tea at six o'clock. Other girls pulled the belts of their tunics tight and slapped their cheeks while they waited at the bus stop for the boys to pass. They spent hours discussing details of the gowns they would wear on their wedding day, how long the veil should be, what kind of flowers. Nora and her best friend could never get interested in discussions of that kind. They had not been taught, like the Australian girls, to make their future wedding the goal and focus of their lives. They had not been brought up with the knowledge that the future was so easily assured. Nora and Maija ate their lunches together: the black bread and salami sandwiches that made the other girls hold their noses. They talked about books and music, about what strange lives some people had had; they talked secretly of how they could travel, whom they could meet. They would be blue-stockings, suffragettes, spinsters. And they might be waiting for someone, but not at the bus stop.

Someone to show them how to be. There were a few women in the orchestra, not many, but there were some. Magda told her that women could be professional musicians, although they were never among the great, and never composed music. Conductors were always men, of course. But women could play accompaniment, and play in orchestras, yes, and this might be her own future. Nora kept secret her intention to be a soloist. A great soloist. She would go to Paris and study with Nadia Boulanger. She would discover a way to be that she had not yet seen, discover something to do that they had not heard of here.

At the School of Music there was Eduard von Kronen, who knew all about all the things Nora most wanted to know. She took lessons in the evenings at the School of Music. There was only one way to get to study directly under von Kronen, and it was a long slow way. She had to pass Preliminary Theory in the first year of her study, and she did; Advanced Theory the next. Three years of studies in Harmony and Aural Training followed. Nora worked constantly, consistently, Magda was concerned sometimes, but Nora ate well, slept well and never faltered.

In her Leaving Certificate, Music was the subject she passed with distinction, and she won a place in the full-time, three-year diploma course at the School of Music. She would watch Eduard von Kronen rehearse the orchestra! And after two years she would win a place in his Master Class.

12
MIGRATIONS—PATRICK

Experience on a country paper was the best training he could ever have. So Patrick was told by Dick Pilger, the Editor. And if he finally got to the city he'd appreciate it.

Getting to the city was exactly what he intended. Meanwhile, Patrick was sent out to report whose cows had won first prize at the local agricultural show and who had relatives staying with them; how much the street stall for the hospital auxiliary had made and which local lady had the best hat at the races; who got married, who had babies and who died. He reported the local candidates' meetings and the visits of relieving clergymen. He went to the scenes of accidents, he went to the scenes of crimes: to his regret there were very few of either. The biggest fuss the paper ever covered was a dispute about whether the town's celebrations for the coronation of the radiant new Queen had been adequate. Patrick got to know the local cop, he got to know the mayor; he got to know everyone in that town, and never took sides in local disputes.

Country people were great readers, at least of their paper, and studied it to the last word on the last advertisement. Patrick learnt to check his facts—on the local news, at least, which had to be strictly accurate or he'd hear about it. As for world news— few people knew the difference.

When he was fourteen, the local paper had run an essay competition for schoolkids and Patrick had won. From then on he knew what he wanted to do. As soon as he left school he was given a job on the paper.

Patrick bought the city newspapers when he could and dreamt of working in the big city office, with its telephones constantly ringing, excitement, bustle, scandal. He would move with ease among men of power and women of beauty, he would know what really went on in places that mattered, he would write front pages that would make the city stop short with astonishment.

He finally migrated to the city, although no one wanted him to go, not his mum, not his dad and not the Editor, who understood best why he had to go.

'Police roundsman,' Dick Pilger advised him, 'get onto that and you really know what goes on. Good luck, son. Keep your mouth shut and your ears open. Ask questions all the time, and don't bury your leads.'

Patrick's first job was to cover the shipping news. Arrivals. Departures. Expected Arrivals. Expected Departures. Overseas ships in port. Every day. And then, making his routine calls dutifully but keeping people talking a little longer for the practice, and with a bit of luck, he managed to be the first to find out about the threatened strike by the union of ships' captains. 'THREAT OF COASTAL SHIPPING TIE-UP OVER PILOTAGE' said the headline. The dispute continued for many days, and Patrick covered it, until the final headline: 'SHIPS PUT OUT TO SEA ON COURT ORDER'. And then Patrick was able to move into the area of the paper he wanted.

'You get thrown in at the deep end here, son,' said Col O'Brien, the senior police roundsman. Col was the kind of man who made being in his thirties look middle-aged to elderly. He spoke with relish of the sins of the city, always pleased to have his sardonic, cynical view of life confirmed.

A school bus had smashed, and three or four children had been killed. 'Out we go, see the parents. These people have just heard their daughter's been killed. You sympathise with them,' Col explained on the drive out, 'ask the parents, or ask an auntie, if they've got a photo. Come back and say she was a top scholar, shame she was killed on her way to her auntie's. You know, you read the stuff. You'll have to do a lot of things that might worry you, on this job. Police generally get stuck with notifying the next of kin. But sometimes we get there first. Our cars are connected with the police cars, fire and ambulance.' Col told

Patrick all the worst things he'd ever had to do, and watched his reaction. 'So you reckon you can handle all that?' he asked.

Col took him to the morgue, he took him to a gruesome car smash, he took him to a little house in the suburbs where a man had shot his wife through the head then shot himself through the head. 'Heard someone or other was shot round here,' said Col, all mock-nonchalance, to the cops who were already at the house. The old cop looked Patrick up and down. 'Aw yair,' he drawled, 'he's not too good. Come in anyhow. Go in, son,' he said, and winked at Col. 'That'd be bits of brain,' he pointed out when they were inside. 'Don't know which part of them that would be.' Patrick went outside after a while, but he hadn't run straight out.

'Okay, you'll do. I've checked you out anyway,' said Col. He had rung Dick Pilger, and he had rung the Inspector of Police from Patrick's home district. They'd said he was a nice young bloke, smart too, go far.

Col took Patrick to the daily morning conferences at the Central Investigation Bureau. 'Hiya Frank, how'ya going? G'day Trev, how is it?' Col would greet the detectives.

'Col,' they'd say. 'G'day mate.' In their greetings there seemed to be something besides acquaintance or friendship—some kind of understanding, some complicity.

'They'll want to know about you,' Col explained. 'They'll see you around for a while and they'll say, "That Patrick Morris there, how's he?" "Aw you can trust him," I might say. I *might*. Till I get to know you I can't vouch for you.'

It was all word of mouth, Patrick learned. He couldn't produce any documents to say it was all right for the detectives to talk to him. It would take time to build up the camaraderie that very few newspapermen, including Col, had with some of the Ds. 'There's only a few who are really trusted,' Col told him. 'You build it up. They start off by saying, "How'y' going?" One day, they'll tell you right out. You'll have to go up and say, "Do you mind telling me . . ." And they'll say, "You're right, mate, we know you're sweet; the position is this, you can't say it's come from here but this is what happened." '

It is police roundsmen who *make* a paper, Col told him. They write the stories that most people want to read, especially in the afternoon papers, like the *Daily Mail*, but all the other papers too. Watch people pass a newsstand: an accident or arrest on the front page will make them stop a lot sooner than some announcement from a politician, or some earthquake disaster from overseas.

According to Col there were certain people everyone wanted to read about, and they came in two kinds: those who wanted to keep their names in the paper and those who wanted to keep them out. Often it was the police roundsmen who got the story.

Patrick decided he would become one of those who got the story. And he knew that this ability would depend on his eventual mateship with a couple of detectives.

If you were trusted, they'd tell you the most fantastic things, things that'd lose them their jobs, not in twenty-four hours but on the spot; they'd show you confidential files, things the press was never supposed to see. They'd tell you what you could use, and if it were off the record you never used it. If you did report it, it might be a good story, but it would be your last good story. If you ever did the wrong thing you were out, might as well go to judge cat shows.

Messiter from the *Post*, he'd been all right. Then one day he'd written up some confidential information, about the truth behind rumours of a bribery scandal, that the Commissioner had told a few pressmen. Messiter had said, along with the rest of them, that he accepted the information in confidence. 'Then bloody Messiter comes out with the whole story,' said Col. 'Never could work it out. Up to then he was trustworthy. They'd told him a thousand other things, now they won't tell him what day it is. I had a violent row with him, naturally.'

Friendships were cultivated in drinking sessions—you got your important background that way. Cops drank with their informers and with a very few reporters.

Six o'clock closing meant nothing to them. You'd hear 'time, please, time; it's six o'clock' in the bar, and the cops and the reporters would move into the back room. 'Bloody coppers, the bludgers,' a departing drinker might mutter as he watched them go inside.

The day came when, after a meeting to tell the press the latest on the dangerous sex maniac on the loose (women warned to lock doors), one of the detectives turned to Patrick and said, 'How about you, mate, are you going to have a drink?'

13
THE BOOK

The last time Isabel sees Eduard again is in '52 or thereabouts. In Australia. 'Aust-RAL-ia, not Austria.' She goes there to do a concert, which he conducts. The first time they had worked together was '. . . oh, never mind how long ago,' she says, twisting a bangle on her arm. 'A long time. I was very very young; he was very accomplished. He helped and inspired me. I knew him before he went to America.

'Yes, so, Australia. It's not somewhere you expect to go, is it?' While the arrangements for the tour are being made, while she prepares herself, and during the long tedious journey, she does wonder about Eduard. How strange and amusing, she thinks, that at last, after all these years, she will see him again. She is going a long way, and alone. They will both be there in that remote city. They had once got along exceptionally well. Will they ever be alone together?

She is met very nicely at the airport by a gentleman from the Australian Broadcasting Commission. He is something high up in radio. 'In Australia,' she explains, 'the government broadcasting establishment runs the orchestras, one in each city. It actually works quite well. Keeps us in a job!' This is all explained to her by the Australian Broadcasting Commission man, Neil or Neville or Norris or something, as he drives her to the hotel. It looks like an awfully drab town, but he says, 'Wait until you see the harbour,' and he is right. You have a different impression of the town when you see the harbour, pretty bays and hills, rather like San Francisco.

Her hotel is in the centre of town, and he says that from there she might enjoy a nice walk down to the water's edge. She can't do any such thing, of course, not knowing what effect

63

that strange climate might have on her voice. She tells Neville all the different ways a singer must look after her voice; he is fascinated.

Yes, there are flowers and a card from Eduard waiting in her room at the hotel. You could never find anything wrong with Eduard's behaviour. With his manners, at least.

And how is Eduard? she asks. He is happy here, she is told. She knows that in America he hated having to suck up to rich art patrons as part of his job. Like Mahler in New York. In Vienna, they say, no one could order Mahler around, not even the Emperor, but in New York he had to submit to the whims of ten ignorant women. It's still the same, those *parvenus* who buy their way into society, then onto some committee, then tell artists what they must play, what they must compose. Eduard is happier with the Australian arrangement. Here, Eduard controls the programs, everything. 'You respect your artists in Australia!' says Isabel to her bemused host.

Norris needs no persuading to stay for a cup of tea, and he tells her that he loves the recording of the Negro spirituals that she has done. And that he is so looking forward to the Mahler at the concert. He loves Mahler! That's what he says. What do these English colonials know about Mahler? Love Mahler—what is it they love? Eduard has conducted some notable Mahler concerts here, she is told. Eduard has created quite a craze for Mahler. Neil seems proud to know Eduard and talk of him. But Isabel also senses some reservation. She suspects that Eduard is not well understood.

She tells the Australian Broadcasting Commission man she must have her rest. He will call for her again, how nice, how kind, how nice.

At the rehearsal she sees that Eduard has a core of devoted players, really dedicated. A couple of them play very nicely indeed. A few of them should not be tolerated, but of course she understands that replacements would be hard to find in such a tiny place. And they have absurd unions here. She saves her voice, at the rehearsal, frightened that the long journey has tired her.

64

She has only a day to recover. She has travelled longer than one day to get to Australia so she thinks she should have equal recovery time. But the contracts were completed a long time ago, and she has nothing to gain from making a fuss. She will save her voice and do her best.

Eduard's behaviour? Well, he does acknowledge that he knows her perfectly well, socially and professionally, and so he does, but he gives no sign of any intimacy. Eduard always had that utter detachment, without actually being cold; always courteous without ever being *involved*. Isabel suspects he drives a lot of women mad that way.

Eduard has always been attractive to women, of course, but their time together in Paris was very special for both of them. A unique communion. No man should be able to forget that, even if there were a marriage or two since then, and whoever else. Look at me, thinks Isabel, if it was something really special I don't forget it. Of course, you must take as much care as you need to, not everyone has to know everything. Eduard was always so discreet.

At the concert she sings, oh beautifully, the heartbreakingly lovely *Das Liede von der Erde*, and, although her attack was a little breathy at one point, she is not unsatisfied.

There is a reception after the concert. The ABC man drives her to the party. They cross the harbour, over a large bridge, and pass through vast sprawling suburbs to the north. Sydney seems very spread out, for such a small town. This is the 'north shore' area, he tells her. Although it is so far out of town it is the fashionable place to live, the 'nice' place. The von Kronens live up this way too. To think of Eduard now living in the nice, respectable part of town in Australia! He used to have a sense of humour.

They have big houses, big gardens, lots of space. You could live there very comfortably, Sydney, only it would take two days by air to go anywhere; unthinkable. It feels a little like being in England. Different from England, too: something to do with open spaces, it changes people. Like English people in Africa,

65

you know? Here they ask her the same kind of questions: what does she think of Australia, is it what she expected? She tells the usual lies: very charming, very friendly, I expect nothing.

She had in fact known nothing about Australia, only that it was at the end of the earth, a British colony, strange animals. She knows more about South Africa (lions, diamonds). This amuses the north shore party; they like to be told that they live in a faraway provincial hole as long as in the next breath you assure them it is all quite up-to-date in every way. Really, for all the practice and study and anguish, it is not the concerts that are the hardest work.

She is very curious to meet his new wife, Marguerite or Mademoiselle or Madeleine; she's not good with names. Apparently the wife has been talking about going on another trip to Europe soon, to take the younger daughter—her stepdaughter—to school in France. Imagine, says Madeleine, the child plays with the children in the street and is picking up an Australian accent! There are sighs of sympathy from her admirers. If anyone could be offended by what she is saying they do not say and she would not notice. Or care.

In the von Kronen Sydney circle one does not speak in a 'real' Australian accent, least of all the women. One is supposed to sound as English as possible. But not everyone is charmed by Madeleine's attitudes. It is said pointedly that one does not need to send children to French convents. There are good schools here that take perfectly adequate care in the matter of accents and manners. But then Madeleine does have French blood and perhaps anticipates living in Europe again, they say. Perhaps Eduard could not be expected to stay here forever, they say. After, what was it now, six? seven years? he might want to go back. He goes back every year! others say. He keeps himself and us in touch with the world.

Everyone who is not talking to the von Kronens is talking *about* them. These Sydney parties: small town, music circles, orchestra gossip, you can imagine. You know, the usual things that are said. That it is time for an Australian to take von Kronen's position and it is well known *who* could do just as well, *at least* as well, if only he had a chance, which, being an Australian, he deserves a good deal more than Eduard. What Australian stands a chance in the shadow of the celebrated Eduard von Kronen? The overrated Eduard von Kronen, it is whispered— Isabel hears this, or senses it; she senses that here in Australia it does not do for foreigners to overstay their welcome and show off their cosmopolitan manners and international connections.

Eduard would stay here indefinitely, others say: after all, he goes abroad every year and has a very good life here and he likes it and it is lucky for them that he does.

Oh, the people there make a fuss of Isabel too, yes, they keep asking 'What do you think of Australia?' or 'It's a long way, isn't it?' or 'Have one of these? Another drink?' Most of the men stand together and most of the women stand together and Isabel is in the area where they cross and meet. Apparently this is the Australian custom.

Possibly the von Kronens are not the only really interesting people down here, but it is Eduard she is interested in. So she listens and watches closely. What is Eduard up to, why does he stay here, will he return triumphant?

Mademoiselle, she can see, does not like it here so very much, in spite of the gushing pronouncements she dishes out to the press—Australian women are the best dressed in the world, that kind of thing. She would adore to know that her marriage was much discussed. Until she finds out that the relentless interest of others in one's personal life is not always so much fun.

People do talk about the von Kronen marriage, that is clear. They do not expect the von Kronen marriage to be what their own north shore marriages pretend or aspire to be. The von Kronens stand apart, they have a certain cachet. He is not a family man. She is his third wife, a much younger wife. He, so charming, yet so aloof. She, glamorous and travelled. People like that—the ordinary rules do not apply.

Isabel will hear, quite some time afterwards, that Madeleine did go to Europe, and that some Polish count, who had arrived penniless in Australia just after the war, left at the same time. The Pole went to work for Radio Free Europe in Munich; Madeleine helped him get the position through her contacts. Some people said this proved that Madeleine was connected with the American Secret Service. That is outlandish of course but it could have been true. It happens. Perhaps that's why she married Eduard, *they* wanted her to go to Australia. You know the Petrov defection? We heard about it in Europe, Isabel will say. Isabel has been to Australia now and she knows how it was. Everything was cold war, cold war, just like America, and there were some small-time Russian agents who defected in Australia, 1953 or '54 she thinks—a cause célèbre there in those days. There was a rather sleazy chap called Bologowski or Balailalski or Bialoguski. He was a kind of double agent for the Australians—they had started their own secret service! He persuaded this Petrov couple to defect and reveal all the Russians' secrets. This Bolovsky had actually played in the Sydney orchestra under Eduard and it was said that he'd won his place there because of Madeleine's influence. He was an indifferent musician, Isabel believes.

No one in Sydney knows anything about all that yet. On that night, at that after-concert supper, Madeleine has not yet left for Europe for the last time.

Eduard arrives at the party, late. Typical. Not even for effect, just his typical vagueness. He had *forgotten*, can you believe it, that he was meant to go there, and had gone home. Madeleine knew him well enough to call their house when he didn't turn up on time.

Isabel isn't insulted. She knows him well, too. She has only the briefest moment to say something private. 'I remember Paris,' she says, 'though let us not remember how long ago!' Perhaps they could tell each other what has really happened since then. 'Have you changed, Eduard?' she asks. Perhaps she only intends to ask, because he never tells her, he tells her nothing.

She sees that he is not in love with his new wife. He is not in love at all, and still he is not so very interested in her. There is a weary look deep in his eyes. He looks so . . . unsatisfied.

She has an intuition, a feeling of tenderness. Take care, she wants to say to him, take care of yourself, and be careful.

There is only one thing that night that arouses his interest. The host of this party is showing a book, a large-sized book of illustrations, to a small group of people. 'She is second rate,' a woman named Margaret is saying as Isabel joins this group. This Margaret is a wealthy widow who collects works by living Australian painters. The host has read about this book and has obtained a copy. As a curiosity, he explains.

'Well, they were right,' someone says, 'it is obscene.'

And other people look at this book and say:

'An artist cannot be obscene, only a good artist or a bad one.'

'The obscenity of one age becomes art in another.'

'Oh *art*! But this! This is not art.'

'Why not? Whether or not you like it, that's a different question. But it's art.'

'She can draw, though; technique. She was taught by Norman Lindsay, wasn't she?'

'Lindsay is overrated.'

'Underrated.'

'My dear, he is a true original.'

'He is a true vulgarian, although he does have technique,' Margaret says. 'He is not what is happening here in art. Since Nolan and Drysdale exhibited in London, Australia is interesting in so far as we provide new images that are recognised abroad as something distinctive, different, uniquely Australian.'

'But Margaret, all good Australian artists are influenced by Europe, as they must be, for we are Europeans here.'

'This artist of yours was arrested for obscenity a few years ago in Melbourne. Some professor or doctor testified that to be Satanic is not necessarily to be obscene!'

'It is very ugly, that is its obscenity.'

'It is frightful rubbish, don't you think, Margaret?'

'As art,' Margaret says, 'it is pretty worthless.'

'Oh you were kind enough to call it second-rate a moment ago.'

69

'Excuse me, but what *is* this? Should I know?'

'She hypnotises herself to do these things.'

'How do you know?'

'Oh, they write about her in magazines.'

'What magazines, we've never seen that kind of magazine.'

'Look at this one, ooop, we'll skip that one, ladies, you didn't see that.'

'Oh don't be stuffy.'

'It is horrible, art should be . . .' (gestures of hands to heart, uplifted eyes).

'She is a witch, you know.'

'A witch, what rubbish.'

'Oh it's well known. She lives at Kings Cross and holds black masses.'

'Stewart, how do you *know* these things?'

'The train on the way home, one sees the afternoon tabloids over shoulders: murder, the races, and a witch in Kings Cross.'

'I went to a seance once . . . yes, table-rapping, and a glass slid round a ouija board, no one pushed it . . . it happens, it's well known.'

'I knew someone who . . .'

'Did you see this, Eduard?'

Eduard, now standing near Isabel, has a quick glance through the pages. Some little recognition or interest sparks in his eyes. He notices Isabel glance at a page. 'A messy, symbolist kind of thing, isn't it,' she remarks.

'The symbolists, like the expressionists,' he says softly, as if he were obliged to comment, 'are not interested in representations of the world around them, but in expressing the essence of Nature in a new language.' How like him: he will not say if he liked it, only make a clever, obscure remark in the most natural way.

Eduard hardly says another thing, and everyone is getting ready to leave, or, if they are the type to become more excitable at the end of a party, are distracted with chatter about poltergeists and mind-reading.

Madeleine, who has not been near the display of the

momentarily curious book, is signalling to go home and making sure the right goodbyes are said. She compliments Isabel on her singing, expresses a hope to see her again, and says farewell to her quite graciously.

Isabel will have to go back to Sydney after the Melbourne concert but nothing will happen between her and Eduard, nothing.

That rather sweet man Neville something looks after her. He has complimented her not only on her singing but also on her appearance. She had worn an ice-blue fishtail gown for the concert, and changed into a black cocktail dress for the party. He arranges for someone to drop his wife off after the party so he can drive Isabel back to her city hotel.

14
THE VISIT

Her book would bring him to her. She wanted to know how and exactly when, too, but she was not allowed to know that.

Human beings should not think they control their own lives.

Her book proved that. A book had been a faint, distant possibility for one future day. And then one day a benefactor had come to stand bail for two young vagrants—she and Terry the Poet. He thought he'd give them some work, and that turned into the three of them working together, getting the book produced.

And then her book was finally out there in the universe. 'The greatest stir since *Love Me Sailor* was banned in 1948,' one of the papers proclaimed.

Her book would bring new people into her world, into her mind. She would meet Someone she had to meet. Someone out there would see her drawings and thrill with wonder or recognition. Someone would contact her and provide her with a further chance to gain knowledge, to understand what she knew.

She wrote letters to England, and sent her book with them. She wrote to a world-famous writer. No reply. She wrote to the most famous scientist. He never answered. She wrote to the leading specialist in the occult arts. Nothing.

Letters came. Letters from strangers. Someone wrote saying he recognised in her work the tradition of fantasy, of other worlds, imaginary worlds; he himself was a devotee of science fiction and thought they might meet to talk about distant planets and their messengers sent on spaceships. She put the letter aside then lost it.

Letters came from would-be occultists who wanted instruction. She never answered those. Letters came asking for spells to gain money or revenge. She threw those out. Letters came offering her commissions. A man wanted her to reproduce the black panther painting but to make the woman in its embrace a likeness of his wife. She never did that either. A man from the Pakistan embassy asked if she would do a book of drawings of erotic paintings in temples. No, no and no! Did no one have any idea?

Timing, that was it, she had to know about time and timing, the unfolding of events in patterns and sequences that you could not and must not control.

She painted at night, she slept by day. She cared for Terry, who had a period of intense neurasthenia and became more frail and nervous than ever. She cared for him as tenderly as if he were one of the animals. A cat had kittens near the Himalaya coffee lounge, and she rescued a lizard from the park.

And then there was the letter from the conductor.

He had been struck, he said, by her vivid and fascinating pictures; they were unlike anything he had seen in this country. Her sense of line, of design, seemed to him most superior. And the content fascinating, reminiscent of certain European surrealists and those whose main concern was not to illustrate everyday life but to explore the psyche.

Eveleen read this letter over. She stared at the name and return address. She thought hard. She had heard about him. He outraged people. Was he the one, she asked? A teacup rattled furiously in its saucer. Yes. He did not play the safe, familiar tunes.

Wasn't there someone who used to sit in the Himalaya with her, someone who had played in the orchestra and gossiped about the conductor? And the papers . . . she did not bother to read the rubbish they put in newspapers. Music, the orchestra, petty fusses about outraging with overly modern works.

Music. She had not been to a concert since she was a little girl. These days, her wireless was usually at the pawnshop or on the blink. When she was growing up she had drawn pictures to music, and her creatures like spirals of smoke had danced and disappeared. She looked again at this letter. She heard a few strains of an ethereal sound and from the half-finished canvas

73

on her easel a ram-horned satyr raised himself further onto his hind legs.

She thanked the conductor for his response and his interest, and invited him to come to see her. Perhaps he would like to see some new paintings? She was indeed interested in the relationship of art and the unconscious, and she read a great deal about this and related matters; whatever she could find. She lived at this address, she worked all night, so he might come at night, or for afternoon tea.

Soon after, she received a brief note. He would like to call on her at five o'clock on such a day, please write if it were not convenient.

He arrived exactly at five, dressed in an English suit of impeccable cut, looking about him at the door. She saw at once what to many women had been a fascinating, or disconcerting, discovery: that the air of disdain was worn by a very diffident man. He was shy.

She did not come to the door to shake his hand but remained on her seat on the bed as he entered the basement laundry where she lived. She knew him at once. In spite of his expensive clothes, his aristocratic demeanour, what she offered him would not be found too squalid. He had visited some very grand places, you could tell, and still he could sit at ease on her stained cushions.

'Ah,' he said, looking at her huge mural, 'Pan. The god of the earth.' The crouched horned creature on the wall gazed back at the visitor, leering companionably.

'Most people say, oh, the devil,' said Eveleen.

'Pan represents what modern man fears in himself,' Eduard suggested.

'Yes quite. Modern man represses what is natural, because of fear.'

He sat among her dusty bones and skulls and bric-a-brac and drank tea from a chipped white mug. She knew he was pleased no one else was there. Pleased, too, to find a striking-looking woman with an educated accent and intelligent voice. She had woken not long ago, and had pulled on a man's suit.

Her relaxed, loose-limbed posture gave her an off-beat elegance. Her high pointed eyebrows sat over a direct gaze from slanted eyes. She expressed her opinions forthrightly. A bohemian type.

A bohemian. For whom the life of art meant a rebellion against respectability and a struggle against penury. She read and thought and painted; she had a bold and precarious life. She knew he was pleased that she would never ask him, 'What do you think of Australia?' or 'Why don't we really talk any more?'

When she had been a child at school, she was telling him, she had produced an illustration of Saint-Saëns's *Danse Macabre*: a huge triptych. On it had cavorted the 'macabre' creatures: vampires, werewolves and zombies. She had given these monsters the faces of her teachers! She had been expelled from that school.

Her attitude to authority was no surprise to him. He laughed. 'I recorded the *Danse Macabre* here in Sydney only last year! The dread tri-tone. *Diabolus in musica*. Some people still claim to faint at the sound.'

'Some ladies claim they would faint if they had to see my pictures,' she said dryly; it was a bit of a boast.

He coughed his amusement. And the creatures she drew, he asked, were they influenced by something she had read, had seen? She had studied, he believed, some writings?

On the occult, yes. And found in them, over and over, an experience of recognition, of coming across something once known, and buried, somehow, among all the forgotten knowledge of this life or lives before it . . .

Ah, no, he did not think her weird or mad, nor would he ask her for spells or divinations or answers. He had already an interest in these things.

And the mysteries, she said, were not only within, but without: the many forces and many beings we humans went about oblivious of.

Did he misunderstand her? Weren't such images projections of the mind? Was it not the faculty of imagination that concerned her, the astonishing ability to create unseen forms, to draw on a storehouse of images in the unconscious, perhaps an unconscious humanity shared: archetypes . . .

No, she insisted, not at all, not only that. She was concerned with awakening the ability to see what was *there*: whatever was hidden by everyday blindness or denial. Actual beings. Yes, she had seen them. For years now her work and efforts had been with methods of arousing or heightening perception. How? Ahh . . .

One of her cats had jumped onto her lap, and she stroked it silently a while, lifting the creature to her shoulders so that two pairs of lynx eyes looked at him. That pose! The image of a woman who cast spells and kept familiars.

What would ensure his need to return to her? Was it just this—her conviction that the mysteries were not to be understood in terms of psychology, as symbols of disorder or as projections of mental states? Her gods and spirits and demons must be respected as existing beings: they were entities that might be apprehended by those who made the effort. Even then, even if your effort were great, they appeared only at their own whim. By grace.

Did he want to discuss the role of the unconscious in art? But she wanted to tell him that Pan appeared to her as clearly as she saw Eduard now.

She looked at him and thought, you will want to hear more from me. What women interest you now? Isn't that the face of a voluptuary under the mask of an ascetic? I will tell you how my methods stimulate the creative imagination and that when you learn from me your art will become as great as your dream . . .

Aloud she asked him where he had become interested in such things.

They were among the many opportunities young artists had in those days, in Paris, in London. You heard the latest music, you went to the studios of new painters, you visited salons, and you were taken to call on someone who practised 'yogi' or was said to do voodoo; it was all part of what was amusing and odd and diverting, part of what one did, because the world was modern.

Dabblings, that was all, he said. One had been made curious by the new influences of different cultures on all the arts—Debussy inspired by the Javanese gamelan, Picasso inspired by African masks. He himself had a thoroughly sceptical nature, not mystical at all, he said. He laughed, and remembered, 'A friend in Paris, long ago, said, "You are a potential mystic, Eduard." I was determined to disprove it. I dislike the sentiment that music proves the existence of God. It proves the fineness of human intelligence.'

These things—symbols, the unconscious and so on—appealed, he believed, to his intelligence, and he did not believe mysticism was a function of intelligence. He suspected it was a betrayal of intelligence. Religion was a betrayal of intelligence.

Eveleen hated religion, especially Christianity with its hypocrisy and moralism. But he must see that religion betrayed intelligence and mysticism both. She thought that Christianity—the church—destroyed rather than nurtured people's sense of the eternal, their natural ability, the senses that had to be awakened for occult knowledge. Eros was sacrificed to Logos and mysticism died.

Eduard listened. She was no fool. She really believed in something. 'How long have you thought this way?' he asked her.

'They took me to a church when I was a baby,' Eveleen told him, 'to be christened. My mother only did it because it was the done thing. As a baby, I yelled in fury all the way through, and spat at the priest.'

Eduard smiled faintly. 'At my christening,' he remarked drily, 'the priest complained I was withdrawn and aloof.'

'Well,' he said, looking at his watch. He rose to leave, and at that moment Terry walked in. Good, thought Eveleen. The young man, who had entered without knocking, paused for a moment as if to assess the disturbances to his territory.

'This is Terry Brown-Leigh. The sorcerer's apprentice. The poet.'

'Ah, the poet, the book?' Strange, dense and mostly obscure poetical writings had accompanied the extraordinary pictures. So they were his? Aided greatly by her, no doubt.

77

He had greasy hair to his shoulders and wore an odd assortment of crumpled clothing, including a velvet jacket of dark red. His eyes were large and deep and dark and he stood there, thin and fragile; he had an effeminate, gamin appeal, almost beautiful, in spite of his grubbiness. He was looking at Eveleen: she gave him direction.

The conductor put out his hand and the poet yielded his own. 'How do you do,' the older man said. 'I am an admirer of your extraordinary co-effort. I am just leaving.' He turned to Eveleen. 'A pleasure to meet you, and I was glad to meet Terry.'

'Yes,' she said. 'Timing is everything. Oh yes, you would know. Good timing is an unresisted affinity with natural forces.'

'Not exactly. Good timing must be practised and perfected. Thank you for the tea. Goodbye, Miss Warden.'

'My name is Eveleen. Please call me Evvi. Call me Hecate!' He nodded and fled.

'The spell of the ensured return!' she said to Terry and cackled. She took five red candles, deepest darkest red, and cast the circle. Candles were lit at each point and one was laid in the centre on a red cloth. On a piece of bark she sketched the conductor's portrait—an outline, an impression; it was enough. This she folded in four and placed under the centre candle. From a box she took certain leaves that were wrapped in an old silk rag. She crushed the leaves and laid them in a little circle around the candle. She stared into its flame and emptied her mind. Then she created the figure of the conductor and began her chant. Later she burnt the bark in the candle flame and then swept up the circle of leaves and let them burn too.

15
CIRCUS MUSIC

Patrick can't understand her sometimes. The radio is tuned to
the ABC, as is usual at Nora's place, and there is some classical
music on. He turns up the radio. She likes classical music, doesn't
she? But 'Oh no,' she says, 'not that, that circus music.'

Nora is in the tiny alcove which is the kitchen, making coffee,
boiling water in a little pot and throwing in the ground beans,
stirring and letting it rise, once, twice, three times.

In front of the sofa, and used as a coffee table, stands the
rosewood chest that accompanied Magda and Nora to Australia.
An intricately embroidered cloth covers it. There is more of the
Hungarian embroidery of brilliant flowers on some cushions, and
some decorated vases on the shelf. But it isn't only these objects,
it is something about how everything is placed, a foreign aesthetic
sense, that makes him feel he is in another land whenever he
is here.

Back home they only ever drank tea. Nora always makes
coffee like this. For him, drinking coffee is one of those things
that makes him occasionally stop and think: this has become
normal for me now! in a way that feels pleasurably odd, oddly
exciting.

He is actually living the life he planned to. Knowing Nora.
He sometimes thinks, when he is all alone and can't help his
thoughts, that he really is quite desperately in love with her. She
is so exactly the kind of girl he has always wanted to know.

He likes her seriousness. She doesn't have the 'sense of humour'
that girls are meant to cultivate. She doesn't feel she has to tell
jokes or giggle. She talks about what she cares about.

He might be in love with her, and does not know what comes
next. He is amazed that no directives from the future come to

79

guide him. Nora might even love him too—although he could not expect her to say it. And yet she never asks more of him than the present. It is nothing like he has ever been told.

'So,' he says, 'there are two kinds of classical music: circus music and the kind you like.'

She laughs. He loves it when she laughs. She is so different from any of the girls he knew back home. Not that he ever had a serious girlfriend there, but where he came from you were meant to pair off as soon as you could. He visited a few girls there; some you'd never be able to get alone in the dark; others they said you could—but you'd have to be prepared to get married soon after if you did. And the highly consequent deed would have happened out the back in the bushes, because there'd always be someone hanging round the house, back home. He might have gone after girls with a bit more zeal, if eyes weren't always on you back there; if he hadn't uncomfortably known girls were taught to see it as 'catching' him; if he hadn't badly wanted to leave that town since his first year in high school. Most of the girls there didn't take kindly to boys leaving town. There were some girls who wanted to leave town, too. But people would always say they left because they 'had to'.

He puts a lot of milk and sugar in his coffee. 'So who was that, then?' he asks, indicating the now quietened radio.

'Oh, Tchaikovsky, I think,' she shrugs. Even he has heard of Tchaikovsky, the *1812 Overture*, one of the few records played on the gramophone at school, cannons firing, all the kids bouncing round in their desks.

'Who is—do you have a favourite composer?' They often talk like this—What's your favourite? What's the best? If you could, would you?

'Well, if there has to be one,' she says, rather shyly, 'Debussy. You remember *L'Après-midi* . . .? The one about the faun? I told you about the poem.'

'Mallarmé, Debussy. I can't even say the names. That was the dreaming one?'

'Yes! Dreaming.' What tender, bewitching mysteries are

80

revealed and hidden in dreams, exactly as Debussy wrote of them; music, as Debussy said, that conveyed 'the remains of dreams in the recesses of the faun's flute.'

Patrick puts his near-empty cup down, and looks across the space between them. Why is she sitting over there? 'So why is he your favourite?'

'His music is . . . perfect. Well, so is . . . lots of music. But it's his . . . style. It's hard, you know, to put music into words!'

He stands, walks over, and sits very close to her. 'There are lots of books about it, aren't there?' He picks up her hand and two hearts dance a dizzy dance. 'What style do you mean?'

'. . . He's French, an impressionist. You know those paintings. Like that.' Impossible to explain the play of lights shimmering in that music. 'And he was interested in painting, theatre, poetry.' For a moment she forgets about Patrick's fingers running tickling circles on the palm of her hand. She wishes so hard to—and how would she ever?—find herself where the arts interchange and work together. And there she herself might find her own voice, her métier, her destiny. Even Debussy, *Prix de Rome* notwithstanding, had not greatly distinguished himself until the original genius of *L'Après-midi d'un faune*. There is time, there has to be time, she has to quell her occasional impatience. 'And he was interested in other kinds of music as well—oriental, jazz. And he would use those too. He's so *modern*,' she says, 'so modern, he makes me want to go to Paris.' She had better quickly finish what she is saying. 'Debussy is so . . .' She wants to say 'sensuous' but blushes before she can. She has spent evenings with some dancers she knows, lying on the floor, drinking red wine, and listening to the sensuous music of Debussy. It gave them all a taste of highly refined depravity, a sense of an elevated wickedness.

Patrick, entranced, runs his fingers over her dry lips, which swell and part into the beginning of a smile, and then he slips them into her hot, wet mouth. Her tongue, with an instinctive seductiveness, runs round his fingertips. He thinks he might die. He puts his other hand behind her head and only gradually withdraws his fingers from her mouth after his mouth has followed

81

them; their kiss is deeper, wetter and longer than any before.

Last time she let him put his hands *inside* her clothes to feel her soft plump breasts, softest softest soft. So she has to now. Last time she ran her fingers over the painful swelling in his pants. Last time, and each time, she let them go a little further. So she has to now.

'Debussy is so . . . hh' he sighs.

'So-ohh,' she agrees, sighing, and he runs his hand up her leg, the black stockings she wears even in summer, the top of the stocking, the suspender button, the suspender strap, the edge of her panties, the ruffle round the elastic, the stretching elastic, the cloth parted from her skin, the moist crease of her groin, the prickly little hairs, fingertips brushing the distant lips, then the folds, the soft heat sticky . . .

The room fills with steam, and both of them moan in pain as she pushes herself away.

'Nora,' he says, hardly able to make the sounds, so hoarse is his voice, 'I don't want to stop.'

'We have to. Now. But not always.'

'When?' he says urgently. 'When?'

'Soon.'

'Promise!'

'Patrick, I *want* to not stop,' she whispers. 'I want to, too!'

16
PRACTICE

If you spoke of God you spoke of the war. Magda says she understands why people cannot believe in a god after those events in Europe: what kind of god allows such an enormity, such monstrousness? How could a god allow a Hitler to go so far? Barbarous cruelty beyond belief—for years after they heard terrible things about what had happened.

Magda also understands why, after what happened, people find their faith deeper and more unshakeable than ever. Such courage, such compassion, such noble behaviour—there were those stories too, there were occasions of sudden salvation.

God or no god, Magda says, it should not make any difference. People are cruel and unjust in the name of religion. People who call themselves agnostic can behave like angels. A good god wants you to be no more or less than a good human being wants you to be. You decide, Magda tells Nora, decide for yourself.

How bitterly and exultantly you search for certain answers and find they do not exist. How urgent and mysteriously saddening it is to wonder about the questions that can only be asked; never, finally, answered. Or maybe only when you are twenty years old.

If Nora believed in anything it was in music, its ineffable, cold perfections, the numinous force that compelled her. She played, she practised: when it was easy and her violin sang, and when it was difficult, and she had to force herself beyond tiredness, beyond an occasional fuzzy despair.

She didn't know what made her practise every day, or why the practice and the learning felt like recovering knowledge she already had, making wholeness out of incompletion.

She practised. She practised her scales and arpeggios, slowly and quickly; she practised octaves and thirds, over and over, she practised double-stopping and vibrato, she played études and caprices. Then after a rest she would practise a complete piece of music.

They say that all arts aspire to the condition of music, the highest of the arts. Music, they say, is the spiritualisation of the sensuous, the sensualisation of the spiritual. In her practice there was endless discovery, in which infinity was glimpsed. Infinity seemed to be found only in the hopelessness of holding onto perfection.

She practised and learned about practice: she must recognise and acknowledge her gains, remember when she said 'I can't do that' and now 'that' is only a well-mastered basis for something new, the next thing she aims to do. But mostly she must be aware of her imperfections, of what is missing. Perfection is revealed in a few sublime moments and part of her practice is to recognise them.

She remembered the experience of this illuminating perfection several years ago. She was still at high school, going to her evening classes at the School of Music. She went to the production there, directed by von Kronen himself, of Debussy's opera *Pelléas et Mélisande*. Little shivers chased up and down her spine from those opening notes: tender, knowing, other-worldly. She was utterly ravished and at the end sat in her seat until everyone else had left the hall.

Some said that it was an amateurish production, compared to Europe; far too ambitious for the resources available, and opera, besides, should be . . .

But Nora had had a vision of what was possible, a vision that might inspire her forever.

And like Mélisande, Nora was without a past, without a country; she did not know how she had got to where she was, she felt she had been done a wrong by an unnameable everyone. Love, when it came, must steal over her as softly as the pre-dawn light, the stillest breeze made by a bird's wing, but as compelling and undeniable as the fated compulsion of Mélisande and Pelléas by the well. And the ring is dropped into the well. Ridiculously, she felt it was her story, and that spooky, angelic music was her own, her soul's own.

She practised, and nourished her faith, small as a mustard seed, that the music would bring Pelléas to her: the poet who awakens her music, the musician who shows her a vision, the fated lover whom she cannot resist.

In the music, as she played, she might discover how to be herself, for no one else could show her. She was a woman who was born into one world and who would live her life in another; who lived in a tiny colonial town and felt she should be in Paris; who would be homesick wherever she was, always, even over the sea.

'Notre mère la mer', as Debussy said, 'the sea is more beautiful than cathedrals.' His *La Mer* was more beautiful even than Paris, than cathedrals in Paris.

Perhaps one day she might discover in herself, as she discovered in the shimmering, liquid Debussy, an equally outrageous modernity and an ability to articulate the unutterable.

She, too, would pass from this raw morning into a luminous afternoon. So far, she played well enough, and understood theory well enough, and performed well enough in her examination, but so far she had not found her originality, her own voice, the work in which she would enter those domains of foam-crested cathedrals.

And she would be shown the way. She had been accepted into Eduard von Kronen's Master Class. She looked the letter over and over. A typed letter, with a handwritten message from him and his almost legible signature. 'Looking forward to working together. Eduard von Kronen.' She stared at his handwriting: the way he formed his letters, the Greek ε and δ. He himself would teach her, he who was like the French musicians he championed—like Fauré, poised and sophisticated; like Ravel, stirring and knowing; like Debussy, sensuous and mystical—even if he never smiled, rarely spoke, and inspired as much fear as respect in the students.

85

If in music she found a kind of religion, and in Debussy a prophet, then in Eduard she found a High Priest.

Patrick had asked her what it was like never having known her father. She had not known how to answer. How different might she have been if she had known him? Any different at all? Nora—men—one day—someone—someone who would . . . would what? She knew she desired something, something that had to do with men. While the other girls from school expected to be married, the people in the world she dreamed of inhabiting expected liaisons and intrigues.

Since she had known Patrick, she felt less and less the urgency of having to go elsewhere, go very far, to lead the life she wanted. Maybe it felt less urgent because it was so much closer. Maybe she was simply happier in her everyday life. Patrick and she could endlessly ask each other: Who is your favourite? What is the best? If you could, would you?

And he had *beauty*—a funny word to use for a boy! She thought of his greeny-grey eyes, his firm, broad body, a sunniness about him, the touch of his hands, the things he did to her, the things he would do . . . It was that which she loved, that openness, that sunniness, that Australian boyishness. He once said, 'Hold this a minute, mate,' and that 'mate', as if she were another boy, made her smile all over. Maybe she was in love, because she now thought her life, because it included him, was already quite wonderful.

She had not let any of the boys come near her before this, there was none she wanted, and then, well, there was . . . it was awful and she usually pushed the thought away before it quite formed. The thought about being damaged.

Men . . . in the shadows of her psyche a murky memory was hidden.

That friend of Magda—he had always received a kiss, for it was normal to kiss in greeting or goodnight. Some of Magda's friends, as they bent to her baby lips, would exclaim, 'She's lovely, this child,' or, 'Noraska, you're growing!' or they would clutch at her and murmur, 'Darling, I once met your beautiful mother.'

86

In later years they would look at her in a different way, a strange, different way—she didn't like it—and they would say, 'So this is what young people like to wear,' or, 'You *have* to wear these black stockings? Then why?' And they would say, '*This* is little Noraska? No! This is a young *woman!*'

And those looks. Then he would somehow receive his greeting kiss on his lips, he managed to do that, and no one else would see. And, it was horrible, and she never never thought about it and would not now. No. But she should. Remember once, so as to know, know something about herself. Perhaps . . . well, so there had been him, that man, that friend of Magda, and thank dearest god he was gone far away now. And he had managed to stay alone with her and he would say come and kiss me Noraska and she did, she did, because how could she say no, she was a child, even if they all said she is becoming a woman now, she could not say no, I suspect you, I dislike you, and he made her sit on his lap, because she had sat on his lap when she was a tiny child, he said so, but it was different now, she knew, and he was tricking her because he made her sit on his lap as if it were the same, as if she were still a child, but it was he who knew most how different it was, with his hands, which would feel her new tender breasts and, horrible, she felt that horrible hard thing of his under her bottom and he made her rock to and fro in his lap, as if she were the little child he used to play with and she *wasn't*, pretending he wasn't doing what he did and the pain of anger and hatred in her now was so great, and she felt so damaged; so damaged by that sly, weak man; by the hideous memory; and by the vengeful anger she felt now that she had let herself remember.

She held her face and wept in hatred and grief and something else.

She was being healed of that, and of all the invisible bruises she bore; healed, and renewed and re-created. She would be in von Kronen's Master Class in a few months, and she would work and work there. If she could gain the respect, the approval . . . and he was so great, so brilliant, was it a terrible arrogance to want

87

his respect? All she could do was to play as well as she could, and then better, always a bit better.

She was still in the middle of her practice. She had done her technical exercises, and she had meant to stretch and drink water in her rest period, but she had sat and thought all these strange thoughts and smiled and wept.

And now Nora took up her violin and stood in her room and played the long fugue from Bach's *Solo Sonata*, and the notes formed a pattern of sublime elegance and precision. Her playing this was a lustration, a purifying flame.

And now, feeling light and pure and filled with a luminous clarity, she would go to meet Patrick.

She washed her face and brushed her thick dark hair and pinned it up. She put a fresh handkerchief in her pocket and pale lipstick on her mouth.

Then Nora crept into Magda's room. Magda was lying down, resting before the restaurant that night. She looked very fatigued. Nora shivered inside to remember Magda crying; 'The tears are falling from tiredness,' Magda had said. Lately they had not been so kind to each other, and Nora realised she had been too absorbed in herself, and had ignored Magda, been impatient with her.

Magda was so often tired lately, and dispirited. She had even begun looking back to the past, and saying she should have taken a job selling frocks, and then opened a dress shop. It was such hard work, the restaurant, endless trouble. Magda would cry a little, and lie down, and speak of her regret, but later she would put on her bright lipstick and rush around again, chattering, organising, doing a dozen things at once. It was Magda who made Nora's life possible. She would be repaid: Nora promised it silently, swearing it to whatever force would hold her to it.

Magda opened her eyes and Nora, at her dressing table, blew her a kiss in the mirror. Nora picked up the bottle of Houbigant, and sprayed behind her ears.

'You are seeing this boy very often,' Magda remarked. It was a question.

'Yes,' said Nora, and didn't turn around. 'He's nice. I like him. We can talk, really talk.'

'Only talk? Can you sit for a moment, darling.'

'What?' Nora went and sat on the edge of the bed, and Magda sat up against her pillows, and said nothing, while Nora wondered what she would ask. Magda did not dislike Patrick, though she was at first surprised that this was the boy Nora cared for after saying no to more suitable candidates. But what, after all, was suitable?

'Do you ever think of getting married one day?'

'*What*? Why are you asking me? You know I don't want that.'

'Not even now?'

'No! No, I want to do so many things. So does he, so does Patrick.'

'We are not bourgeois who say you must be married for sex, and one day you will want that, perhaps already?' Magda said, suddenly, astonishingly. 'You will be legally an adult, how long now?' Magda looked at her and Nora looked at their hands; they held each other's hand tight. How hard it was to say certain things! 'But you have another year of school, and then more study and work, that is still your plan? Good. Darling, one day, and it may be soon, or even far off, but you know you can become pregnant if you are not careful, so let me tell you how to prevent that, yes? And God forbid you should ever need an abortion, but if you ever do, you must tell me at once, because I will know how to help you, and it is better if you do it early. You would ask me, you promise? Give me a kiss. Where are you going? I must get up now.'

17
MAESTRO

You might wonder what Eduard von Kronen thought when he was awarded a knighthood the year before he left Australia. Quite possibly he remembered what Paul Valéry said to Claude Debussy when Debussy was proposed for the *Croix d'Honneur.* 'Every real artist has the power, some day, to decorate the government.'

This might not literally be true, alas, but it is true in a better than literal way. The point is, it is unwise to take too seriously the judgements or actions of governments. You are unlikely to know all the reasons they do what they do.

Von Kronen was sentenced to decoration one year and disgrace the next.

He never did make the Sydney Symphony Orchestra one of the six best in the world. It had been a hyperbolic claim, of course, but he had done more than anyone else might seriously have attempted. He had made the orchestra a very respectable one by world standards.

They say that when he took over, 'It was a ragged little orchestra who had played with Gladys Moncrieff in *Maid of the Mountains*'. Not world standard material.

When he took over, there were women in the orchestra who would take out their knitting during rehearsals, expecting to be able to add a few rows to a beanie or a jumper during the intervals when their instruments were not being called upon. They never appreciated his putting an end to their knitting. For some people, being in the orchestra was just a good public service job: plenty of security, with regular increases in salary until you retired.

Von Kronen also found some musicians there of high calibre, and under his direction the orchestra became one instrument.

He was perceived by so many people as aristocratic, aloof,

arrogant, or any combination of these. He certainly could not please everyone, and he certainly did not. His conducting, many said, or repeated, was 'cold', 'streamlined', 'chromium-plated'.

'As though,' he would retort, 'classics should be played in that fuzzy noisy manner. As though,' he would argue, 'you should sacrifice note values and dynamics to the "romantic spirit" of the music. As though,' he would lecture his critics, 'you should "emote loudly".'

Eduard loathed an emotional response to music, the idea of music as having mainly to do with 'feeling' and 'mood'.

When it was suggested that there was too much contemporary music in his programs, he said that these suggestions came from 'those who would have been the first to resent their local picture houses putting on an unvaried fare of Douglas Fairbanks Senior in *The Three Musketeers*, or having their newspaper serials consist entirely of reprints of Charles Dickens's work.'

He often answered his critics in interviews or in the 'Letters to the Editor' column of the morning paper. He spoke out on matters musical, and matters related.

'Parochialism is an ever-present danger,' he said. 'The incapacity to see ourselves internationally as others see us. It is a poor compliment to Australians to suggest that a minimum of one tenth of one per cent of the newspaper space devoted daily to racing and fashions could not be allocated to the pulsating daily activities of the community's artists and musicians.'

While, as the principal conductor of his orchestra, he defended his choice of programs and his directorship of the orchestra to his critics, to those who criticised his compositions he did not reply.

Of his oratorio *New Heaven and New Earth*, one critic said:

'It lacks drive and force and most of all invention. Whilst to the physical feat one must pay tribute, there is little to be said for its musical significance.'

And another:

'. . . his response to the prophet's heavenly visions is music of lively distinction and sentiment, yet missing the kind of ecstasy

91

that a Mahler so often comprehends in comparable music.'

And:

'He belongs to that middle rank of composers who have great technical skill and knowledge but who fail to discover the striking musical ideas needed to print their creations indelibly on the mind.'

Enough of critics. No one knows who these critics are today, while von Kronen is still respectfully remembered. Not principally as a composer, true. As a conductor, as a champion of the contemporary and the experimental, as a major influence on a society redefining itself.

His taste and reputation for modern music brought a new generation to concerts. Von Kronen had already begun the concerts for schools, and then he instituted a 'youth series'— a concert series especially for those under twenty-five. The youth of Sydney responded wholeheartedly and were photographed and interviewed huddled in sleeping-bags and blankets in all-night waits for tickets; lines of young Australians, old and new. They read books, played cards and sang, waiting to obtain the best tickets for the new concerts, the Youth Series. The kids really went for the colourful, bizarre, exciting music of modern composers.

No composers write ahead of their times; it is only that audiences are behind theirs, or so it is said. The older, established audience would ensure a sell-out of concerts of Haydn, Brahms, Beethoven, and they stayed away from the moderns. As if there were not an enormous amount of dissonances in Beethoven. As if . . . but logic has nothing to do with it.

Modernity is what Eduard trusted in himself. *Il faut être absolument moderne*, as Rimbaud said, and Eduard responded to this directive: he knew that he himself *was* modern. He was in Paris with Diaghilev in the '20s. He had met Debussy, his idol. He had founded his own orchestra especially to play contemporary composers who were being ignored: Stravinsky, Ravel, de Falla, Schoenberg.

Many years later, when he came to Sydney, he encouraged the playing of these same composers (still outrageous), and of

Bartók, Delius, etc. He staged a daring production, with a modern, impressionistic set design, of *Pelléas et Mélisande*, full of the mysteries of innocence and guilt and bottomless unexpressed tragedies. He conducted many of the great symphonies of Mahler; Mahler was not being played much, even in the rest of the world. And Wagner? In the 1950s? So soon after ... But yes, Wagner must be played, he was a great musician and those who try to taint great art by associating it with ugly political doctrines must not succeed. Besides, the past is past. And all the Jewish concert-goers came to the Wagner programs too.

Eduard von Kronen seemed to be a sensual man, beneath his austere surface, yet his appreciation of music was never expressed in sensual or emotional terms. He was not someone who was ravished by the *sound* of music, the sensual experience of that sound, its emotional or spiritual referents. How, then, to understand him? To what extent did he 'love' music? Did he love music at all? What did he love in it?

Possibly he 'had an ear so precise that he heard through the sound to the structure'. It was the *structure* of music, the structure that quickened and vitalised and transported him.

Leibnitz said: 'Music is the hidden arithmetical activity of a mind that does not know it is counting.' But Eduard *heard the counting*.

But some musicians who still talk about him do not agree with this theory; they say he was more instinctual than that.

During the concert season of his last year in Australia—although he could not have known that it was to be his last—Eduard von Kronen collapsed while conducting a Bartók concerto. He was rushed to hospital, and of course his collapse was reported in all the newspapers. Soon he had recovered, and he went on to complete the season. When you look back on it, though, you wonder if it was not a portent of a far worse disaster. But then no one would have thought of Eduard von Kronen as a man who was inviting disaster. He seemed to be a man who was prepared for the future, one with an assured future; and he did make his mark on the future.

When he returned to Sydney for the last time, the city had recently been invited to inspect an exhibition of designs submitted for an international competition. From the time he first arrived, Eduard von Kronen had insisted that the city needed a new building for concerts and opera, and he made sure a lot of people began to think so too, and the competition was his idea. One site after another was inspected and seriously considered. Then finally, on a jutting peninsula in the city, covered in old sheds, for it was the site of the tram depot, the perfect site was chosen. Among the designs was a breathtaking futuristic drawing of a building made of sails billowing as if filled with sea air, a building that could float on the harbour waters and stretch its white arcs against the brilliant sky.

18
BECOMING A WITCH

'You look like a witch!' The first one to say it had been your mother. You had painted your eyebrows to slant up your forehead, and you'd painted your eyes to exaggerate their natural feline tilt.

And you're a bitch, you thought, calmly. You were fearless but you did not say it aloud. There would be slaps and tears and wails and sobs, and there was nothing to gain from that. You would never be a nice little lady for Mummy and would never learn to draw pleasant pictures. 'The garden, Eveleen, should give you inspiration,' your mother used to say hopefully. You might try to make a drawing of the flowers, she would suggest, perhaps a dear little kitten playing at the edge of a flowerbed or looking appealingly scared up in the branches of that nice leafy tree down the back. Your mother wanted you to make pretty pictures and then do your face nicely and one day meet the right kind of boy . . .

'You look like a witch,' you would be told again, later. You had left art school and you had left home. You were free to indulge your predilection for outlandish apparel. You wore what you wanted: it was considered bizarre. Your eyebrows now were permanently plucked into their minacious slant, your hair blackened and cut to show your pointy ears. You wore billowing blouses, mannish suits, animal-skin prints. You were fond of your leopard-skin shoes, and a piece of leopard-skin fabric which you wound round your slim waist. You walked with an impatient self-possessed stride and you looked upon others directly. They said you filed your teeth to points; they said, 'There goes the witch.'

95

You did not conform, you did not mince about in pastel dresses; you were an artist, you were who you were. People stared at you in the street, and you'd give them something to stare at. You didn't think much of people, anyway. You'd start to care what people thought when they had half the honesty, loyalty and wisdom of the animals you genuinely loved.

People. Stuff them, you thought. A witch! Bloody nonsense. People called you a witch because it was a word for what they feared and misunderstood.

Since you were a child you knew you had special gifts. As you grew older you began to investigate the meaning of these gifts. You became a student of the range of disciplines and beliefs known as 'the occult'—the hidden. You read about hypnotism and symbolism astrology numerology demonology and divination. You read about reincarnation and extrasensory perception. You read about the Buddha who sat under a tree and received enlightenment; about the third eye, about poltergeists, about monsters who had walked the earth, about gurus and hermits on mountain tops and elixirs that bestowed immortality; you read about sorcerers and shamans and magic. You looked up necromancy conjuration invocation incantation and the witching hour. You found out what you could about talismans and amulets. You studied archetypes: symbols of the collective unconscious, and discovered them in your own work. You drew pentacles; you read about tantra; you studied astrology: the configurations of planets, their transits and conjunctions; you learnt about the lines of the hands, the secrets of numbers, the seven principles of hermetic philosophy, the ten Sephiroth of the Tree of the Qabbala, the eightfold path of Buddhism.

You learned of the pagan religions of early mankind and of primitive people who still practised their timeless rituals in faraway lands. You sought material on the rites and rituals of those with a love for the natural world, those who knew of the many spirits that inhabit this living earth, from which, they knew, they themselves sprang as naturally and rightly as did trees and rocks and mountains. Did you ever consider that they have been ignored

96

and neglected and forgotten, those myriad spirits? That ancient spirits were left behind by white settlers, and the spirits of this conquered red country were still unknown?

Mostly, you had no one to guide your explorations. Your readings were random and eclectic; your conclusions instinctive and certain. You had a natural ability for trance and you received knowledge from other planes. Beings appeared to you at random moments. As you drank and took your pills and painted throughout the night, sometimes they guided your hand, the brush over the canvas, and sometimes they made you loosen your clothing and open your legs and arch your back and remember the most primal rites of connection.

You needed to know more. There were books, which came your way by a natural magic, but books were not always enough. So once in a while someone would come to you, and pass on some knowledge you could not otherwise find . . .

During the war a million American troops passed through Australia. Australian girls learned to say 'Hi!', they learned how to get a pair of nylons and they learned the jitterbug. You met Cherami and learned about different things. He was an American soldier from the South. He actually liked the way you looked: your scarlet blouse with man's trousers, your leopard-skin scarf.

He spoke to you in a beautiful voice, its entrancing rhythms rich and musical. Where he came from his people kept their African traditions. He told you about voodoo and obeah, the rituals to appease the spirits. Some of his people would have nothing to do with it, ignorant superstition they called it, or devil's mischief, and they followed the white man's ways. But in his family the grandparents had passed it down. He had been to these rituals, he had been possessed by spirits. He remembered nothing of it afterwards, but he had seen others so possessed and knew what happened. Ooohh, the drums and the dancing! Sex, this was sex squared, sex to the limit but more than sex; you'd drown in your own juices! Colour, drumbeats, spirits, sweat, naked glistening black skin, possession, chanting . . . oh, and this was *occult* too,

97

driven underground, secret, sacred, insiders only.

And you learnt other things when you walked about the streets with Cherami and sat in cafes with him. There was the way people looked, and what they said, because you kept company with the black soldier. He was black, black like the night, black like the secrets you knew, black like the spaces that welcome the brave. How people hate what they fear and fear what they don't know! It proved to you that most people's opinions were quite worthless.

You wanted to find a master who would teach you to develop your gifts. You had learnt all you could from all the books you found and from anyone you came across along the way. You needed a great teacher, a guide.

'Are you a witch?' people had started asking you, years ago. Trouble with police began, and courts; an exhibition had been closed, paintings were seized, trials held, and reporters from newspapers and magazines came to see you. 'Devil worship . . .?' they asked.

'No,' you had told them, 'no,' you would sigh, sometimes exasperated, 'I am not a witch'. You wanted to answer them seriously, let them understand. 'The devil is a Christian god. We have never heard of the devil. I am a student of art and of philosophy. I experiment with states of mind. I know how to go into trance so that I can paint the universal symbols in the unconscious mind,' and they would write down what you said and admire your paintings. You did look odd, but you were not a witch, they'd sometimes decide. For witches were cackling old hags with warts on their noses. But the editors of newspapers knew their job, they knew what a story was. They would print a picture of you sitting under your paintings of Pan and call it 'Black Magic at Kings Cross'.

Pan was half man and half goat, a pagan god, a faun, a god of nature and music, a lusty lifeforce, the Elemental. He played his pipe of seven reeds and seized many a nymph in his carnal hold. He was the horned god, a friend of pagans, and, when he played, his cohorts would throw off their clothes, sing and dance and take one another in a joyful, abandoned embrace. Pan and his followers were graceful rosy creatures who lived in union with nature's forces.

Then came the Christians: pale and terrified, hate-filled and repressed. They had crucified their prophet who taught forgiveness and tolerance and the inner divine, in order to mock his name with their religion of bigotry and rigidity and stinking hypocrisy. They looked upon Pan, who represented all they feared, and they said evil! Satan! witchcraft, the devil!

It was because you, Eveleen, loved Pan—who had appeared to you many a time by now, and came to admire the paintings you made of him—that the whiteys called you a witch. That was their word for their ignorance. So ignorant were they, that they had persecuted and tortured innocent women in bygone times, and, in a modern way, still did.

Witchcraft, you believed, was an ignorant word. And to prove it you went to the State Library and searched its catalogues. W. Witchcraft. 'A sorcerer is one who by commerce with the devil has a full intention of attaining his own ends.'

That was the opening sentence of one of the Inquisition's textbooks. It was quoted approvingly by more recent writers, apologists for the Inquisition. They claimed there was sufficient evidence of diabolic practices to justify the actions of the Church in cleansing the world of anyone involved in, even suspected of, such practices.

You read the accusations of vile pacts made with the devil and with demons, of obsession and possession, of succubi, familiars, witch's marks, sabbat rites.

> . . . the witch as she really was—an evil liver; a social pest and parasite; the devotee of a loathly and obscene creed; an adept at poisoning, blackmail and other creeping crimes; a member of a powerful secret organisation inimical to Church and State; a blasphemer in word and deed, swaying the villagers by terror and superstition; a charlatan and a quack sometimes; a bawd, an abortionist, the dark counsellor of lewd court ladies and adulterous gallants; a minister to vice and

99

inconceivable corruption, battening upon the filth and foulest passions of the age . . .

Is that what they think you are, Eveleen? Listen to the tone of sermonising moralism, the frenzy of outraged decency, which informs these accounts! You've heard those voices and they were talking about you! These are your kin, then, spoken of in this way. Don't you crave to know more about the knowledge and practices of your ancestors? Don't you think you might have a gift for that kind of thing, powerful secrets, secret powers? Powers, that's what you have, you must learn to develop your powers.

There are modern-day witch-hunters and they warn you, they warn all fortune-tellers and clairvoyants, that they should know of the dangers and perils that the mere possession of such faculties exposes one to. They heap up their warnings and cautions, and advise all to shrink from such manifestations. You would shrink, they say, if you had any idea how easily you could become a prey of controls and influences so cunning, so potent for evil, as to merge body and soul in untold miseries and shadows darker even than the bitterest of deaths.

With what relish these warnings are expressed! Don't you itch, Eveleen, to defy all the forces that might battle for control of your power?

Turn to some different books on witchcraft. Gentle, rationalist voices. Let us make a definition. Let us say witchcraft is a Christian heresy limited to western Europe. Rationalists speak of the witch-hunts of 1450–1750 as a shocking nightmare, a foul crime, the deepest shame of Western civilisation.

Psychology and humanism in the age of science combine to point out that there never was and never could be such a thing as witchcraft. Witchcraft was a crime that was impossible for human beings to commit. It was the purely innocent who were so horribly tortured and slaughtered in the name of Christianity: harmless old women who lived alone—perhaps they talked to themselves, perhaps they kept a cat for company. Anyone who

100

could swim was condemned (and tortured to death), for swimming showed the person had renounced their baptism by water so the water refused to receive them. If the test proved their innocence, they drowned (but went to heaven). Also suspect: anyone with an unexplained mark on their body, anyone who happened to be passing when the milk went sour, anyone who had predicted a storm, anyone who might be blamed for any baffling phenomenon of the natural world, or named by an enemy for spite or for revenge. They were tortured until they confessed; silence was taken for guilt, and confession consisted of forced assent to the lurid and detailed descriptions composed by the Inquisitor's assistants. Thus all the orthodoxy of witchcraft's practices (the rationalists point out) was invented by sexually repressed churchmen.

Imagine them, novice monks and junior priests, who had taken their vows in a world of few available professions, enforced thereby to lifelong celibacy. No sex, ever. Just because there weren't any jobs. They were men after all—many doubtless with faith of dubious resilience—and they had no expression for their maleness. They were thoroughly schooled in the most misogynist philosophies ever devised: taught that women were feeble, childish, avaricious, faithless and sexually insatiable. 'All witchcraft comes from carnal lust which is in women insatiable,' said the bible of the witch-burners, the *Malleus Maleficarum* of 1480. When a woman thought alone she thought evil. She could become a witch. She could become a demon who aroused the sleeping male to ejaculation and stole his semen. The monks would sweat over their manuscripts by candlelight, febrile fantasies fuelled by the discomforts of denial and the strict injunctions to produce the dread documents that would damn those who were made to own them. We who are modern, we know what Freud said, we know about neurosis and psychosis, repression and projection, we know whose confessions they really were!

Thus the church constructed the devil, even to his tail and hoofs and pointy ears, his immense, scaly penis, and his cohorts kneeling at his backside to bestow the foul kiss. The Church

101

invented the rites in which Satan's cohorts opened themselves to all his embraces, unimaginably vile as they would be were it not necessary to recount them. Pederasty, sodomy, bestiality— endless variations on the sex act, created by untrammelled imaginings, truly impressive in their inventiveness. The witches cursed the godly and cast spells, and their familiars sucked upon their teats. They caused nuns to throw up their skirts and scream obscene invitations to copulation. The Church created volumes of confessions, these rich tales of horror and imagination, and millions died horribly to validate them.

Well, Eveleen, what do you think of all that? Doesn't it prove to you that your pursuits will be most reviled and most misunderstood by those who have most to fear? Doesn't it prove that the people who call you a witch want you to express *their* most hidden desires?

Four-fifths of those prosecuted for witchcraft were women. Because of the misogynist fantasies of males? Because of the desperation of powerless men confronted by forceful women? Because the conflicts were domestic and therefore casualties were of course mostly female? Or because women were actually dominant in subversive movements, then labelled diabolic, later labelled Dianic? Those were questions for later inquiries: Eveleen gathered their essence: that witchcraft was condemned by the kind of people she hated—those who hated and feared women, nature, sex, passion, mystery.

The rationalists, then, say that real witches never existed. But what about the powers?

You looked among the dusty shelves of the public library, and found the nineteenth-century writer named Eliphas Levi. Although demons, he says, were in fact only the imaginings of Catholic monks who forced themselves to avoid copulation, 'the secret powers you know are raging within you have indeed always existed'.

Yes, Levi claimed, there had existed, and there still was, a potent true magic, and yes, there was a formidable secret, and there was indeed a unique imperishable dogma and yes (yes

102

Eveleen pay attention this is for you) there is a science that confers on man prerogatives apparently superhuman.

'Here I must pause,' says Levi, 'and I already fear that I have said too much.'

To know this magic, to conquer and control it, to have that power—don't you long for that, Eveleen?

You kept on reading. An ordinary reader might have been easily deterred from much perusal of the occultist writings available then. They have a suffocating density. Levi and his ilk composed their tracts with deliberate obscurantism; they have a self-important solemnity that might baffle or irritate an agnostic reader.

You were no agnostic. You were a believer.

There were, Eliphas Levi claimed, transcendent secrets that medieval adepts concealed under such more or less equivocal expressions as the *Magnum Opus*, the philosopher's stone, the quadrature of the circle, the universal medicine, the transmutation of metals. And he has unravelled the secrets. He has discovered, *in fine*, the secret of human omnipotence and of indefinite progression . . . he is the Master of the Absolute.

And you, Eveleen Warden, artist, reading these precious volumes in the public library or curled up on the raggedy red velveteen spread on your studio bed, vowed, in all your passion for what was possible, with the craving to extend your vision beyond what even your visions had shown, vowed that you too would become a Master of the Absolute.

You discovered Margaret Murray, whose ground-breaking anthropological study, *The Witch Cult in Western Europe*, in 1921 said this: 'Underlying the Christian religion was a cult practised by many classes of the community [which] can be traced to pre-Christian times and appears to be the ancient religion of western Europe.'

Murray gave an account of the chief festivals of this cult (an imaginary cult, according to others), called Wicca. The feasts and dances (the 'obscene Sabbat') show that Wicca was a joyous religion. *A joyous religion*, Eveleen! A women's religion! A religion

103

of ancient feminine knowledge and celebration! 'As such,' says Murray, 'it must have been quite incomprehensible to the gloomy Inquisitors and reformers who suppressed it.' The burning of witches was 'sacrifice for the incarnate deity' of this Dianic cult, and Joan of Arc, for example, belonged to this ancient religion, not the Christian one.

Now you know who you are, Eveleen! You are a witch in fact, an inheritor of an occult religion of reviled women. Women have genuine powers of healing, women have rites, inherent gifts and knowledge, which have been belittled, scorned and denounced by conquering patriarchs; women have been able to live alone, unmarried, unprotected by men: a state that has invited the deepest revulsion of all. The Christian church was a religion for men, men who feared the ancient powers of their grandmothers—feared them so much that they devised and imposed the most gruesome tortures in history on countless victims.

You belonged to a historical sisterhood. You were a Jew, you were a black and you were indeed a witch, a witch after all. You would learn to practise witchcraft, and, proudly and assertively, *you would be a witch*. Now when they came and asked you, 'Yes!' you told them, proudly. 'Yes, I am a witch.'

19
MEETINGS

She had moved house soon after their first meeting, and, knowing there were more meetings ahead, had written to him with her new address. He wrote and proposed a time for his next visit. He arrived punctually. She heard his knock on the door.

'Come on up,' she called, 'I'm on the balcony.'

She heard him at her door. 'Here,' she called. He went through the room cluttered with her objects, a new Pan mural half-completed on a wall. She had lit a couple of candles in bottles. She lay naked on the balcony, with her legs wide apart. She was dripping condensed milk from a can onto her clitoris. A kitten was licking it off. 'Sit there,' she said. There was a chair opposite her. 'There is an important energy chakra located in the genitals,' she said. 'I am currently engaged in a program of exercises to keep my body in a state of constant sexual excitation.'

He sat, composed and patient, watching as the kitten licked her. Then Evvi lifted the little creature, caressed it, and let it go. Then she told Eduard about Sex Magick.

It's not just sex, but an enactment of a union between two deities. Not symbolically, but really. The Great Rite is part of the third degree initiation; the priest and priestess take the role of god and goddess and join together in union and become one. Taking the role is not a mere acting charade: the Deities are invoked so that they are channelled and made manifest in the man and woman who know them. She, Eveleen, is a High Priestess and can make him, Eduard, a Priest. She is empowered to initiate him. When he is ready.

The sexual ecstasy is to be transmuted into the magickal fire which feeds the ecstasy of being united with soul, and it is to stimulate

105

the magickal imagination that one is in the arms of the manifestation of one's own Divine Lover—the Guardian Angel, the directing and protecting Daemon, the heavenly Bridegroom.

The magickal imagination! From this faculty comes all inspiration, all artistic creation, and when you let it rise you then can create as the gods create! Eduard said, 'I have been waiting to meet someone just like you; I have been waiting to meet you.'

How he wanted what she offered! How well she knew that. He had been cautious at first, he was so anxious that if they were to have a liaison it would be above all discreet. He had to learn to trust her; and he had to learn that she was very important to him. And he learned to help her too; he could bring her the things she needed, things she couldn't get in Australia. He went to London every year.

She had promised him the one thing he would sell his soul for: artistic greatness, the renaissance of his greatest power. She knew that together they could create magic that would make them both great, great artists, great magicians, as great as the Great Beast. She had felt such a certainty at their first meeting. And before that, when she had received his letter. And before that, when she had only heard his name. She always knew, yes she did, that he would need her and together they'd raise powers that would make the outsiders fall to their knees.

They soon found that they were destined to create a great work together. Eveleen happened to mention the fact that once she had painted sets for a theatre. A left-wing fringe theatre—yes, he had heard of it. The company had needed a set for their big last scene, one to look like hell itself. She had painted the set in a single night's work and they had been delighted with it.

How auspicious, how fortuitous, Eduard said. Did she happen to know the stories of Edgar Allen Poe? Yes, Poe's stories had always been particular favourites of Eveleen; she had first read them while still at school. And yes, *The Fall of the House of Usher* was one she knew well. She delighted in its sense of an unnameable menace, the palpable presence of the kind people call supernatural, although it is as natural as people.

She, Eveleen, Evviwitch, understood so well the appeal of this powerful, sorcerous story. He had learnt so much through having written and finally conducted his own oratorio *New Heaven and New Earth*, based on the famous vision in the book of Revelations. It had been received—he shrugged—well enough. And he was ready to go much further in his next work.

Well, Eduard had always had it in the back of his mind that one day, when the opportunity came, he would like to write an opera based on *The Fall of the House of Usher*. Claude Debussy had always wanted to do this—Poe's story had been an inspiration to him as had Mallarmé's poem for *l'après-midi d'un faune* and Maeterlinck's play for the opera *Pelléas et Mélisande*. Debussy had worked on it over the years but had died before it became a reality, and all the music he had written for it had disappeared. And now Eduard wanted to do it. Now, he needed to find a librettist, and there was someone from America who would be perfect. And he had always thought that it was most important to work closely with a designer. A designer, of course, who had enthusiasm for the work, and a vision that harmonised with his own.

And she was the one! If, that is, she . . .

She certainly did. It was a perfect idea. Only, she said, the librettist should be Terry.

'He is a wonderful poet,' she said. 'He and I understand each other. You and I understand each other. Surely you two will enjoy working together.' Eduard wanted to think about it. 'It is meant to be,' she insisted. 'We three will be tightly bound in magic. We will use the highest form of magic together, the three of us. And then the power of our work! The magickal fire,' she reminded him. Superior art comes from a superior imagination. If imagination is a magical faculty, as any reflection on it will reveal, then magic is the way to cultivate, to improve, to refine the imagination. He must agree. The three of them would work together, in magick and in art.

Eduard gave her tickets to his next concert. When she and Terry arrived the concert had already started. They heard the faint blurred last passages of a piece of music as they stood and waited outside the large carved wooden doors. What was it? She didn't get to hear much music these days. Terry the Poet and Eveleen were allowed in when the piece had finished. They crept in while the audience was applauding. Not bothering to find their reserved seats, they sat in the empty row of seats along the back wall.

She looked down the length of the hall full of human heads to the orchestra, and there he was, coming back onto the podium, powerful and dignified, to take his place before the players.

He raised his arms, and there was a moment of deep concentrated stillness. He raised his arms like The Magus. There was stillness; all breath was held still. He gestured, and there was sound. His gesture created sweet melodic sound; sensible, ordered, complex sound.

He was a true channel for some force, non-material, unearthly, divine, abstract, complex. He was the centre of a vortex of powerful energies. Each element of the music existed only as potential until he gestured, and made it manifest. He transcended his human personality: his identity, all he was, was the music he made. 'Magic is the science and art of causing supernormal change to occur in conformity with will' and what he did up there, in that hall, with more people paying him breathless attention than ever they paid her, that was magic.

20
BONDI

Patrick came in and watched her for a few minutes before she saw him. The Two Cities had been busy that night and Nora was helping out.

Now she was his, and yet she remained unpossessed and always would. How well he knew her now, the creamy skin, the slightly oriental slants of her face, the curves of her lovely body underneath the large shirt, the tight, checked skirt, the black stockings. No, he would never know her completely, she would always surprise him.

She had surprised him when, after giving herself to him, taking him completely, she became troubled and restless. Wasn't she supposed to become contented? Did he do something wrong?

She waved him over to the staff table near the door to the kitchen. 'I won't be long,' she said. 'Take some coffee if you want,' and she hurried on through the door.

The musicians—piano and violin—were finishing a gay little polka, and a couple on the tiny dance floor was twirling round and ended their dance on an answering flourish. As the duo on the tiny podium began its last piece, a slow, shmaltzy last-dance-for-me number, the couple moved into a tight formal dance-hold and swayed dreamily in time.

Magda was talking to a table of regular men customers, who had just finished their dinner. Patrick was unable to hear what they were saying, but the pantomime showed clearly that they were, as usual, pleased with their meal. It was a table of men who spoke in soft voices, Australian men with an exaggerated gentility, who smoothed down the linen of the cloth with fussy fingertips, twirled their wine glasses in the light and spoke and laughed very softly, as if no one should ever overhear.

Patrick remembered the first argument he had had with Nora, right here, watching those same men. 'Poofters,' he had said. 'What's wrong with that?' Nora had asked. He looked at her in astonishment. Men like that, 'light on their feet', as the saying went, 'a bit musical', had been objects of derision among all the men he had ever known. You should never wear white socks in case people thought you were one! They had secret signs, like the Masons. He had heard of a man who had killed himself once he realised he could never change his homosexual nature. 'Poor bastard,' people said, but there was the feeling he was better off dead. There had been a stir earlier this year when the staid morning paper had printed the word 'homosexual' for the first time ever.

'What's *wrong* with it?' Patrick had echoed, as if even asking were unbelievable.

'Prejudice,' pronounced Nora with the same scorn she reserved for those who wanted statues covered with fig leaves (though she still hadn't taken off all her clothes for him, had she?). 'Prejudice, ignorance.' A tiny flash of guilt told Nora that she was only echoing what Magda had told her. But she knew Magda was right, she thought, because the way she spoke of it made more sense than this uncharacteristic outrage that Patrick was now displaying.

'Homosexuals, it means,' Patrick said. 'Do you know what that means?' Unspeakable practices, moral corruption, children in danger. A faint shadow of a yet-unformed thought hovered on the edge of his mind. Later, the thought would fuzzily, teasingly appear. It was a suspicion that something about all those things he had been told about homosexuals, something about the *way* those things were told, could not be trusted.

'Of course I *know*,' said Nora. 'Homosexuals have been great poets and artists and . . .' And dear friends of Magda, but, untrusting, she did not say that. 'And they don't hurt anyone, and it's natural, and the ancient Greeks thought it was the highest form of love,' she added desperately.

'Ancient Greeks,' he said, serving her scorn back to her. 'The

110

ancient Greeks. That makes it all right.' If only he knew some unsavoury barbarism committed by the ancient Greeks, but the ancient Greeks had produced democracy, the Olympic Games and marble statues . . .

Col O'Brien would tell Patrick with relish of the raids police made on homosexuals' private parties. Col, being hand in glove with a detective or two, would get the story and write it with moralistic outrage, as if these parties, as if the very existence of men who had sexual tastes different from his own, were a threat more dire than the atom bomb. When Patrick had to begin to ask himself if the homosexuals were really hurting anyone, if these raids had any justification, or was it perhaps Col who had something wrong with him, these questions were as big a challenge as moving to the city had been.

So when he had that conversation with Nora, they had leant away from each other a while, with a disappointed mistrust in the icy space between them.

And later they were close again, talking into the late hours, incompleted thoughts tumbling out into the happy opportunity of sharing them, fragments joining into fresh young beliefs.

Now, tonight, in the Two Cities, Magda moved away from the table of regular men—and Patrick had nothing against them at all, he had to admit that now—and came to say hello to him. She was as elegant as usual in her black hostess's dress, the silvery-blonde hair in a chignon, the expressive hands moving as always, the face, the bright red lips, gaily animated, then, in repose, changed to sombre lines: fatigue, worry; never for long. Magda was usually in motion. She kept on going, to keep on checking that everything was perfect at every table. Perfectionism, thought Patrick; she and Nora are alike.

Patrick glanced around and noticed the couple at the far table. He looked again. He looked harder. 'Magda *neni*,' he called to her, 'who are those people?' Magda didn't know. 'Er, I think,' he said, with diffidence, for Magda was busy, 'maybe you should ask.' Magda looked at him, then went to check with the new waitress who had served them.

111

The woman had come in and said she wanted to take her fiancé to a special dinner that night for his birthday. Unfortunately, it was already after six—but what was a special celebration without wine? The waitress had understood perfectly, she had been very nice to them and had let them have a bottle of wine with their meal. 'They looked like good customers,' the waitress said.

'They haven't paid?' said Patrick. 'No,' said Magda, and realised what his concern was. 'No? Oh no,' she said. 'Oh God. Kerry,' she called to the waitress, 'you haven't given the bill to table number eight?'

'I just put it down,' Kerry said, and Magda almost ran across the restaurant to snatch the bill out of their hands.

Nora, curious, came over to him. 'The happy fiancé,' explained Patrick, 'is a copper. I think the woman is too. Doesn't it make you feel safe,' he said with heavy, furious sarcasm, 'to know that the police are keeping the streets safe, keeping us safe from criminals, getting themselves up in plain clothes to save us from dangerous people who *serve wine* in their restaurants?' They looked over to table eight. Magda was insisting that the wine was on the house, she absolutely would not accept payment for it. Because it was his birthday, and she gave the big thwarted man a thin, cold smile, and came back to the staff table with the bill, and sat down to write them a new one, and sent it over with Kerry.

Magda had had trouble with the police ever since she first opened and had told them she could not afford to pay them the £50 a week they wanted. She was already paying £50 a week for the lease, and it was a lot of money. Some big-eared man named Sergeant Mould from the Vice Squad had come in. Years later, she heard he was the new head of the squad. Aptly named. She was very young—not yet thirty when she started—and believed that all she now had to do in life was to work hard and be honest. 'We'll get you,' the police had promised, and they did.

She had made the restaurant a success through her own work and the owners, from whom she leased the restaurant, now wanted her out so they could take over. It was the owners who had brought in that man, who, when she thought about it, had been a bit incongruous. She should listen to these instincts. 'He's from Melbourne, a company director, please treat him well,' the owners had said to her. She had treated him well, allowed him to buy wine from her. He ate his meal, drank his wine, then arrested her. The police declared her establishment a 'disorderly house', and she could not serve any alcohol at all until the court case. She made only enough money to pay the staff and rent until the case was heard. It was with some satisfaction that the case was thrown out of court. 'Judge slated police on move against cafe,' the headline said. The judge admonished the police for keeping from him the information that it was a well-run, reputable restaurant. The application to declare the restaurant a disorderly house was the most iniquitous he had seen, the judge said. 'It reads more like Nazi Germany . . .'

Let's leave Nazi Germany out of it, thought Magda to herself, but she was most relieved.

'You tried to make a fool of us,' the police said. 'We'll get you.' And they kept on trying. And she was tired of it. Her life had been through more changes than most people can dream of. She had had enough of change, she sometimes thought, but if it was time for another one, she would make it. One more year before Nora finished all her schooling—but she did not have to wait until then. She could sell this restaurant now. If change were inevitable, let it come.

Magda looked up from the night's pile of bills, looked around. People were leaving, going home, even the Europeans, even those men. Yes, she would sell this restaurant, then she could go out to dinner as other people did, talk and laugh and gossip and flirt. She knew that the restaurant and her work had been her preservation, her therapy, her deliverance. And now—time for something else. She would return to, no, she would go to a *new*, normal life.

If you could have one in this country. How many more changes would there have to be! Some of her friends said she should discourage Nora from going out with the Australian boy. They wanted their children to mix with, and marry, their 'own kind'. They wanted their children to speak only their 'own language' at home.

'English is our language now,' Magda would say. They argued. They kept giving her advice, the couples, thinking because she was single and not a real mother that she knew less than they. Sometimes, it was true, Magda needed assurance, but it was Nora who gave it to her. There was a time when Nora had been so moody and easily upset and discontented, and Magda feared she would be blamed for it, and even feared she *was* to blame. But no, it passed, it was all part of growing up. Even if the moody periods returned, as today. Because of the boy, probably.

But Nora, however moody she became, never became lazy. Magda was thankful that the child had determined her own direction very early, for, while she gave Nora all the support she could, she did not think she could have found it in herself to force Nora to do anything, and she did not think Nora could be forced.

Some of the married couples did push their children, pushed them hard, so that their achievements would compensate for their losses. Others were so jealous of their own children's secure opportunities that they undermined them constantly.

What did you do with the past? How did it fit with this life?

Magda thought of the friends who expected, when they arrived in the antipodes, dispossessed as they were, that they would be invited, welcomed, feted, by the Australian upper classes. The Australian upper classes had no interest in them at all. The Australian upper classes were all nouveau riche and descendants of convicts, her friends then said. They did not come from very old families with very old names, who had honoured their old obligations as they should.

Magda got tired of such talk. Does the past matter?

With those for whom it mattered, the same stories were retold. Long sleeves hid tattooed numbers. Or sleeves were rolled up to display the tattoos. Old blood married new money. Doctors

114

and professors laboured, shovelling dirt. Countesses became housekeepers for convicts' daughters.

Those who cared so much about the past forgot that even in their own countries—what used to be their countries—'Baroness' meant nothing: you bought the title, or you built a railway.

Does the past matter? If so *how* does it matter?

Magda almost jumped out of her chair, so startled was she, when Nora put her arm round her shoulders. 'Deep in thought!' said Nora. 'You go home now. I'll finish everything here. Go on.' And, for once, Magda did.

Nora had noticed Patrick when he came in that night. Although she was busy carrying a pile of dirty plates to the kitchen, she had looked over to the door, as if she had been made aware of his presence. How beautiful he looked, golden fair, the freckles on his tanned face, those strong upper arms of his—her discovery. No one had told her how thrilling an upper arm could be!

Could she explain to him, oh dear, could she explain to *herself*, why she had withdrawn from him? And after they had been so close, as close as two people could be.

And that was nothing like anyone had told her.

Not even Magda, who had in effect given her 'permission', even said there was help if it ended in trouble!

She meant an 'illegal operation', that's what the papers called it, and the girls at high school had whispered about the dreadful things that happened when you let a boy have his way. If you led him on and didn't stop him soon enough, firmly enough, it was too late, and he forced you, unable to help himself, and hurt you, and then would despise you and leave you; and if you got into trouble, oh! awful things, you would have to leave school and people would know, know why, and you would have to have an illegal operation, which cost hundreds of pounds, if you could find anyone to do it, which would be worse, as they were evil people who did that and could damage you inside forever and you would bleed to death or never give your future husband children, even supposing you could hide what happened and if anyone would ever marry you; or else, if you got into trouble, you went away and had it and adopted it out and it would haunt you forever, and what that would do to you. If a girl went too far everyone would know and oh! oh! those things whispered about you, those awful words. 'Free love is cheap love', that's what the papers said. (But there was the world of difference between cheap and free.)

That was at high school. At the School of Music—perhaps there was more of an idea that people made different choices about these things. *Other* people. But it still wasn't that different from high school.

Strange how certain ideas seemed to be related. It didn't make sense but the lies about sex, the way they seemed to want you to hate sex, or to be afraid of it, all that seemed related to the way the police kept trying their little tricks to book Magda for serving alcohol. If the law changed soon, then something illegal one day was legal the next. What a stupid, terrible world.

Nora sent Magda home, and Patrick helped her as she cleaned up. 'No,' she said to Patrick's suggestion of going somewhere for coffee.

He walked her home, up Darlinghurst Road, over the big intersection and up the stairs to the little flat in the building near the fire station. Magda was already home, so Nora wouldn't ask Patrick to come in.

'Thank you,' Nora said formally, at the door to the flat, and turned to go inside, leaving him there on the landing.

'Nora!' said Patrick, taking hold of her waist, not to kiss her, only to look at her face, find there if he could what made her so blue, so distant. She instinctively raised her hands, and put them on his upper arms, and how could she then just turn and go? She began to cry, instead, and they sat down on the dark stairway, and he let her cry and then she felt a lot better.

'I can't explain it,' she said. 'I'm glad about everything.' She meant she was not sorry they had made love, which for Patrick was a great relief to hear. He thought it was the best thing ever invented and that once discovered it should be practised endlessly.

116

Why didn't she agree? Well, he had been told that women were complicated.

'After everything,' Nora began to explain (so she was going to call sex 'everything', was she, all right then), 'when I practised, I tried to play, and I was . . . umm . . . all wobbly.' She had not been able to concentrate, and could only think, over and over, of that time, of the day they had gone to Bondi . . .

Patrick had taken up surfing. Nora had never been to the beach. At last he persuaded her to go with him. First she went and bought a bathing suit. She tried it on and looked at herself, almost quite bare, in the long mirror at the shop. She usually wore clothes that covered her completely, black stockings even in summer. Some people told her she looked like a beatnik but she didn't care. She took the tram to Bondi with Patrick, and they were thrown against each other as it turned suddenly down the hill to the beach. Sparkling blue water stretched out to forever. He held her hand and foamy waves massaged her bare body in the new bathing suit. Patrick hired a tent-like beach umbrella, and in its shade stroked oil onto her exposed skin, then kissed her, salty, wet, tangy, and they could have gone on forever like the sea. Next time she went into the water a wave picked her up then dumped her hard, and another wave broke over her, and she was in a tangle, and when she had spat out the sand, and recovered, they screamed with laughter. She was really an Australian now. Patrick went back to the waves and she lay in the shade in a sparkling dream, her skin tingling.

When they came back to the flat they were alone there, they were alone there for hours. They did not stop, three times one after another it was everything, once she was rigid and apprehensive, the second time she relaxed and responded, and then the third time she took hold of him, drew him into her, flowed like a river in flood, blossomed in golden globes like wattle heralding spring, sang like trees in the wind, and erupted with him in a storm of total revelation; and in each other's sweat they were baptised.

117

And then, the next day, she tried to play her music, and could not.

She still felt the foamy waves, the stinging spray, the oil stroked onto her legs, her skin tingling and hot from the sun. And everything.

'You were wobbly?' Patrick asked.

She had not been able to find her still, concentrated centre, and had discovered another primal fear, another fear she had not been warned of, the fear that *everything* did demand its fee after all, and that the price of that joy was her ability to find the silence from which music emerges.

'I thought I'd changed, and it changed my music,' Nora confessed. 'I was afraid. But I'm all right now. I could practise today.' She had played better than ever.

'*I* was afraid . . .' Patrick said, as they sat side by side on the stairs in the dark. He didn't say, afraid that she had turned against him, that something about 'everything' meant she would stop confiding in him.

'Oh no,' Nora said, like a rainbow in a sun-shower, 'it was only me.' So she did not blame him. 'I'm sorry,' she said, 'it's hard to explain feelings, especially when you don't know what they are! Then I was afraid it was too late.'

'It's not too late. I knew it'd be all right,' though he hadn't really. He fervently hoped that her idea that she was playing better now meant that she did want to do everything again.

'Anyway,' said Nora, smiling once more, smiling bright as the waves at Bondi, 'you came to the rescue tonight!' She meant the cops in the restaurant.

'Them,' he said, with a great deal of distaste. 'I've had it,' he said. 'The stupid things they want to book people for.'

Patrick, although he had a mercurial nature, did not want to feel as if the different parts of his life were so very separate. But that kind of thought threatened great changes, and now it was late, and they were both very tired. His new ideas would have to wait, everything would have to wait.

21
THE GREAT RITE: SEX MAGICK

She is waiting for him. The flickering lights of candles create shadows in the darkness, create dancing phantoms on the green glass globe that was her scrying-glass, illuminate the face of the Horned God who leers and grins in delight, cause the skulls and bones that remind of endless rebirth and endless rebirth to shine then disappear then shine to the same candleflame rhythms.

All has been agreed upon. The script has been written and learned; not a word out of place; all is set for a perfect play, a shadow-play, a transcendent reality.

Inside her dusky, musty room, the rickety sofa has been pushed into the centre, east-west. It now stands before the altar, facing south, from which the Elemental gave his blessing. On it she has thrown all her precious, tattered odd cloths—velvet and brocade and animal prints—that in this mysterious half light seem rich and exotic and make a bed fit for gods to sport on, as indeed they will. On this bed lies the scourge, the smooth stick with the many cords. Not a word! Not yet! As arranged. It is the witching hour and he enters, enters the room, to enter, oh but not yet. In the corner he removes his clothes and pulls on the simple robe left there for him. She is clad in a similar robe. These are soon to be removed, for sky-clad the ceremony must proceed. But first, to cross the border between this mundane reality and the greater reality that lies beyond . . .

In his robe he approaches the altar, where she is lighting many thick sticks of incense; the air in that closed room is soon laden with overpoweringly sweet, oriental scents: musk and ambergris and aphrodisia. An old gramophone has been wound up and its needle placed on a record of Tibetan chanting. On the altar, alongside the athame and the white-handled knife, the pentacle, the salt and the candles in their holders, some marijuana cigarettes have been placed beside a large goblet of wine: substances to facilitate the initiate's entry into the illusion, substances to enhance the movement to the realms of the Other.

The wine is handed to him. He swallows and shudders as it burns its way down: some spirit has been mixed into it, and there is a bitter chemical taste as well. Bravely he swallows again. She swallows deeply too. The candle she holds up to her face as she lights the first cigarette shows her slanted eyes glistening bright; she is already high on her speed pills. She draws in and hands it to him; they hold acrid smoke deep in their lungs and swallow the burning potion until their heads rise, up off their bodies, revolving and orbiting in endless dizzy motion.

Each has a task: each has developed a supreme ability to concentrate and, as they swallow and as they smoke, each concentrates on the Other—not as the human beings they know, no, no longer those poor imperfect mortals, but as the embodiment of the Deity, the Divine Lover.

Four candles are burning at the points of the four elements. The circle has already been cast: the consecrated sphere within which they finally shed their human identity through the ritual scourging that purifies the body completely so that the Deity might enter.

The record turns round on its round turntable and the chanting it plays, scratchy, hollow, other-earthly sounds whose notes arch and dip like satellites, is circular too, and the smoke drifts in rings, and his breathing goes in then out but round, round, inbreath becomes outbreath in an endless circle of breath that breathes him, and he sees the magic spirals painted on the walls and feels his whole being go into the same twirling spiral. He kneels, and the lashes of the lustrating scourge caress and sting his flesh in arcs of tender pain.

Heat rises as they remove the robes, and, sky-clad now, begin the invocations. In the measured, poetic language that is pleasing to the gods (and is easier for humans to learn by heart) they invoke their Deities, call them, and with respect and knowledge of them command them to manifest in the body of the man and the woman. He begins his invocation with eyes closed, oh the whirlpool he's in, while she looks right at him; as they repeat and repeat the magic phrases, he opens his eyes, the words turning circles in the air, their bodies, the smoke, the sounds of breathing in the now still room, all a complex of intertwining, dancing circles . . .

Then the sound (from where?) of a mighty rushing wind, a gale that arises in that very room, storms around it in a whirlwind of immense force, a force that is answered by a rising force in the body. The brave little candleflames rise huge but do not go out, and oh yes, look at her, the woman, the woman before you, indeed she is, oh Hecate, Artemis, Isis, Luna! Before you is the Divine Female manifest, the Goddess incarnate, oh and his body is grown straight and strong, broad-shouldered and silken-skinned like a youth in his powers, strong and hard and huge, with a desire a lust a need a power a fierce triumphant raging randy lust, and like Pan himself he seizes the woman, the princess, the goddess, the Divine Lover, his own Daemon, his own Other, seizes and enters and ravages and he takes her and oh the swirls and eddies of their frenzied, perfect motions; she becomes a pulsation, a tender vice, a point of light, taking unto herself again again her dear god her lusty Elemental her vigorous half-man half-goat; he seizes her by the hair and throws her face down, he hammers her delicate centre, he splits her in twain, he grinds himself deeper and deeper within, he is lord of Nature he is Supreme Intelligence, he enters the heart of all mystery. Gods are fucking the universe spins they are planets in the firmament and they cause explosions great enough to create new worlds, he roars like an erupting volcano and the scorching river of larva drowns the earth.

Which heaves great sighs and becomes still. And now it begins.

Now for the greater purpose of this rite: the first matter transmuted to Elixir. They take the 'matter which is neither alive nor dead', the transmuted substance, the spirit made flesh, the Magickal Child, the White Eagle and the Red Lion, the transubstantiation, and they will feed upon the flesh of God. The bodies have parted. Her fingers reach for the still throbbing, gently softening male organ, the Athanor, the furnace; his fingers reach for her sticky lower lips, Cucurbita, the gourd; they take the sweet sticky Nectar, and take it into their mouths: they consume the most holy sacrament, the rejuvenating Quintessence, the Elixir.

And she takes her awaiting bowl. And in the last seconds of divine incarnation she takes from his cock and from her vulva and the drops that streak their thighs she takes into her bowl, the most magickal essence, for using this she possesses the universal key of all Magick, she can make Nature change to her will.

This is only a start, she thinks. You will want more of this, there is more we can do. You will scourge me till my pain becomes ecstasy and you will need to come back to me again and again; you, my Chokmah, my Baphomet, my own Great Beast 666, and from this thunderous union of deities the power will rise in you, power to create to control to make music beyond your dreams, together oh the power to create!

A cold, naked man is lying, robbed and drained, in a dingy little Kings Cross room. He stirs and it is cold now, these coldest, darkest hours. He will leave. He will put on his clothes, and leave. There will be no words. He will leave.

22
THE GREAT RITE:
I WASN'T THERE

The letter arrived asking for her memories of Eveleen Warden and at first she decided to decline. But it nagged at her, all the false impressions that had grown around this much-maligned woman. She found herself involuntarily writing back. Then she proceeded, quite intentionally, with her memoir.

Evv Warden was *not a witch*. She was a wonderful person, a unique individual, a talented artist; she studied many things, she was a natural trance medium and she did do magic. She was not a witch, though. Witchcraft is channelled, and disciplined— and look at this work of hers, this is just chaos.

See these faces of hers—she painted an idealised version of herself, maybe what she could have become. Look at these serene, wise faces. That's what she never achieved, that serenity.

I knew her. I was very young, 19, 20. This was about 1946, '47. We used to draw together. She taught me a lot about drawing.

She was a lovely person, a wonderful human being. She was androgynous—not lesbian, androgynous. She was a slender build, tiny. She was a nature spirit born in a human body; trapped; an embodied nature spirit. More than anything she was a faerie person.

She was very intelligent, she wasn't at all pretentious, and she was her own person. She would not accept others' measure and that was very unusual in those days. 'It's a sin to be different'— she was the first to say it. She was ahead of her time, that was her trouble. 'I am as I am,' she would say. 'I am me.' You didn't hear that anywhere else in those days. Evv was very conscious of not interfering with whatever she was, seeing it as not good, not bad, just what she was.

As time went on, though, I became very cross with her. She let herself go, she lived in filth. I didn't see much of her then. I told her why. She was still very sweet, she'd say, 'Will you come to visit me if I clean up, Anita?'

One day—this was back then, the forties, when I was still going over for drawing lessons—I took over some sandwiches for my lunch. I ate them, and threw my crusts in the garbage. Evvie went over to the garbage and got them out and ate them! I was horrified! 'Don't do that!' I said. 'It's filthy. Why didn't you tell me you were hungry? You could have had one of my sandwiches.' That's what she was like; she wouldn't ask for anything, and she wouldn't mind getting some food out of the garbage. She was always poor. She never made enough money. Yes, her spells would work, a lot of them, but if she made spells for money they didn't work. Maybe people who are legends aren't supposed to be too comfortable. Not that I think artists should starve or any of that rot. You should know what discomfort feels like, but if it goes on too long it's very debilitating; fighting with poverty takes too much out of you, doesn't it, you need your energy for your work. Artists shouldn't starve, they put up with enough to get their work done; they should always have enough to live on without worrying about money on top of everything. Evvi, though, never seemed to have anything at all, she never had quite enough. I wouldn't like to say what that meant.

Oh Evv and her wyrds! They worked though. Once she was on a street corner with a couple of friends and they hailed a taxicab. The cab started to pull over but then drove off—didn't like the look of them. Evvi just lifted two fingers of each hand, like this, and he had four flat tyres before he reached the next corner. Evvi could be bitter and vengeful. Sometimes I think, well, maybe revenge is only reclaiming your honour. Or maybe she did too much wyrding. Curses are supposed to come back to you fourfold.

124

She wasn't a witch, but she was a magician. And a neo-pagan. It's all related. The Craft is very old—some call it the Old Religion. But you're right, it's developed a lot in the last few decades, it's a living, evolving religion. If you want to call it a religion. I call it the Craft, or the Way. Some people call it Wicca. Wicca meant the Wise One; it used to be known as the religion of the wise or the joyous religion. These new books on Wicca—they are modern and feminist, part of a New Age trend. The Craft was feminist long long before any of the feminists! Before the feminists and before the patriarchs. The Goddess is the most important, the central Deity, She is worshipped above all. It is all being revived and is growing now because more and more people are realising that the Goddess is needed. Look at what patriarchal religion has done. Where is the feminine? Who looks after the earth, who keeps us in harmony with Nature? Men don't!

People need a spiritual life and they need the Goddess. Even the Catholic Church realised it couldn't take people right away from their pagan Goddess worship. Father, Son and Holy Ghost—the church councils fought about it then decided the Ghost was male too! But to keep the people in the Church they had to let them have their Goddess—that's why they created the Virgin Mary, who is an aspect of the Goddess. There have been many places where so-called Christians cared a lot more about the Virgin Mary than the Father and the Son. They could talk to her, like they always talked to the Goddess; they knew she could influence the Powers, and she was the one who really cared about their everyday domestic problems. Who cares most about the family, love-life, food, neighbours? Men don't.

In early pictures the Virgin Mary looks proud and strong, authoritative, even fierce sometimes, because she is a manifestation of the ancient Goddess, but later . . . The patriarchal religion made virginity the ideal in women rather than fertility; you see the sentimental stuff, the passive helpmate; she's there only to be a patient, suffering mother, a sexless second fiddle.

The witch was the reverse image of the virgin. A witch is sensual, knowing and commanding. A witch is inspired by the

Goddess, in any of her manifestations.

The Goddess must be part of our lives again. This awareness is growing now. It's allowed to be more out in the open, too, but in Evvi's time things were more hidden, and she had a harder time finding them. You know the Witchcraft Act was only repealed in 1951 in England—much later here in Australia, the seventies—and that's why everything had to be so disguised.

A lot of people are writing about the Craft in a very open way now, not about some things that can never be out in the open, but a lot of it. Others don't like it, they believe in keeping it all secret. You get all these different ideas of course: secrecy or openness, the hereditary witches and the new ones, the Gardnerians and the Alexandrians. Whether nudity is required in working, if the sex should be symbolic or actual, the extent of flagellation. Some covens say the Horned God is an equal Deity but we say the Mother Goddess is paramount. Anyway, Gardner came out in about 1953 I think, and Evv did get hold of that. But most of her study was from the old texts, from the ancients, the classical Greek stuff, the Qabbala; some of the Rosicrucian stuff was around then.

Aleister Crowley? Oh well. Yes. If she was following all his stuff that explains a lot. He was a great magician, but he really got off the track. And they say that he 'booby-trapped' his books of Magick—he'd leave bits out, or change bits; they say the demons like everything to be done just right and if you make mistakes—disaster! I think the word-perfect thing is probably not so important, it's that the intention should be integrated; Evvi's was too dispersed. She certainly was very daring.

Evvi trusted the demons too much—I'm sorry if I'm wrong, Evv, wherever you are now, but she did, and she invoked demons, not only the Deities. That's dangerous stuff. She seemed to think they were all trustworthy, like her animals. But they can be very capricious, they can be mischievous, they can be as wicked as humans. They could have led her astray. Magic should be very disciplined, and dedicated.

I knew a young couple back then, with a baby. They lived

down in Edgecliff, not far from the Cross. They moved into a little flat that had a really malevolent presence living there. Everyone could feel it, you'd just walk in and at once you could sense this evil thing. And everything started going wrong in their lives. So they went and got Evv, she wouldn't ever have had a phone, they went and found her, and got her to come down. And she walked in and said, 'You dear little thing, you poor dear thing, come home with me, come with me.' And she left and it left with her and the flat was a lovely place after that. But that's what I mean about her trusting too much. This thing, or one of the others, might not have been trustworthy, it could have sucked away her energy.

We believe in working in groups, for psychic power and psychic protection. She was very much on her own, Evvi was. These days there'd be more room for her, she would have peers. She taught but she was not taught. She worked out her own rituals and spells—mixed up all sorts of things. She did not itemise the aspects of Deity she wanted, so she got a chaotic, undisciplined power. You must know the weak links within yourself, know them very well; you must know what aspects of your own nature are liable or weak. If you are truly great and you invoke a pagan Deity you would get all the positive force, but if there's a weak link you get the negative side. She lived in a base and sordid way so what she attracted to her was base and sordid. The power you can raise is very great. If you go wild and your judgement goes—you can destroy yourself.

We all need ritual in our lives. The difference between ritual and routine? We like routine too, don't we; our animals like routine, being fed at the same time in the same place. Routine should have a practical purpose, and rituals all come from a practical origin. Nature, seen the pagan way, Nature works in ritual ways: the seasons, the solstices and equinoxes—very important times for pagan ceremonies. Ceremonies all have their own purpose and the purpose of ceremony itself is to affirm our harmony with Nature and her ritual transformations.

Some ritual starts from a practical purpose and then it becomes

127

symbolic. If it's just an empty routine, it's meaningless, but symbolic meaning can be as important as a practical purpose.

They say the old pagans, druids and witches, would keep certain ceremonies to 'ensure the return of the sun'. We now say it is more like ensuring the sun within. We keep the same ceremonies they kept in olden times. We were all once far more aware of the greatness and indestructibility of Nature. We sought friendship and harmony with her, we befriended and appeased her with offerings and sacrifices, we made sacred rites out of her mysterious gifts to us—the seasons, the harvests, and sex. Nature is great, greater than any of us; when we've all gone Nature will still be here. Funny how a lot of people seem to have forgotten that. We all have to remember it now, though.

That's why there's this revival, and these books and the interest. The Mother Goddess and the Horned God are important to us again.

Unfortunately, Evv neglected the Goddess. I think Evvi was *in love* with Pan, in love. She wanted a god to love. Pan is lusty kindly compassionate wise—he's both gentle and strong, the ideal male. She was looking for a god in a man.

Where would she find one? Australia was only a village then. The only people with her were outcasts and freaks. She hated the bourgeoisie, but she would have loved to find intelligent, educated people who had no time for the establishment (we didn't call it that then).

Von Kronen? I didn't know him. I heard something about that. Well, he was an artist, wasn't he, a musician?

Sex Magick—that's not the Craft. You invoke Deities for Sex Magick, you dedicate the power to your poetry, art and music, for the purpose of making the world better. Or else Sex Magick becomes an addiction, something done for its own sake, being only about possession, more like voodoo.

I don't know, I wasn't there. I didn't see her so much in those days, into the fifties. But I could see by the way she looked that I didn't want to be part of whatever she was doing. I'd see her and want to go home to have a bath. Forgive me for saying that, Evvi, wherever you are now. She was a tremendous person, but then she got so cross and angry and power-happy. And she did file her teeth to make them pointy, and her eyebrows got more and more—straight up her forehead they went. It's a shame, isn't it. She used to be a really lovely person.

23
DAYLIGHT INSOMNIA

Eveleen stirred in her sleep. The unwelcome daylight forced its way through the gaps in the curtains. How she hated the vile, bright summer light trying to invade her little room.

God, her mouth was dry, it tasted foul. She reached for a glass, then spat out the sour wine in disgust. She was awake now. Sort of. Her mouth was a dusty desert, her whole body thirsting. She'd better get up and make herself some tea. Was there any tea in the kitchen? Maybe not. Go out and get some? Awake and dreadfully thirsting. She'd better do something. She dragged herself out of bed, her body stiff and painful. Was she getting *old*? How old was she now? She reached the window and clung to it, the room spinning in blackness for a while. Got up too fast. Slowly the room settled down. Thirty-something. It'd be forty one day soon. Thirty-six maybe. Thirty-six *what*? Work it out. Thirty-seven. What did it matter? Other women worried about age. Most women fear their best days are behind them. What the hell was she doing waking up wondering how old she was?

At the age of thirty-seven it's a rare woman who knows it is not too late for anything.

She had on the clothes she had worn last night and had gone to sleep in early this morning as the dawn was streaking the sky. That's as much daylight as she ever wanted to see, thank you. She couldn't see properly in daylight. Things were coming back into focus but she kept leaning against the wall by the window. What had she done last night? Where was Terry? Oh, yes, there had been people here, and a lot of drinking—everyone drank, and those who remained on into the long cold hours before dawn had drunk more, and 'Let's have a ritual!' they said. 'Come on, Evv, let's do one of them masses.' And she had obliged. *What for*? They didn't really know what it was about, or care, the drunken layabouts, and she had begun her invocations. But the Beings refused to manifest, and the people hadn't known the difference, but gathered in the circle, giggling, or a bit spooked if they hadn't been before. And then a bit of general rutting took place, but it hadn't been pagan inspirations, only, yes, there were the empty bottles. And she could even make out the strong odours in the room: stale drinks left in the bottom of glasses and spilt onto the dirty rugs, the butts of cigarettes in piles of ash, dust over mounds of odd objects, unwashed clothes, the droppings of rats in the cupboards, the rotting secretions from human bodies, the sourness of her unwashed body—she smelt when she'd been taking pills . . . The pills! Her dexies! Where were they?

You felt terrible when they wore off. You felt so low, so sick and jittery, you dragged around, the air tasted vile. You didn't know how you would ever bother to do anything again.

She had a good supply at present. She'd done without her dexedrine for a while; she couldn't get any. Drinking wasn't the same. Smoking wasn't the same. And she had missed her little dexies. They started out only as an embellishment: an added fillip to her natural energy and exuberance. She would swallow the little pills and soon her pulse would race, her heart beat, her mind fly, her imagination soar. Paint leapt onto her brushes, the canvas reached out to them. Her creatures peeked out from all corners; her studio would be populated with their sound and presence. They would guide her hand and the paint would swirl onto the canvas in entranced, ethereal spirals and spheres.

Then, one day, she realised she never had as much energy without the pills. Any energy at all. Well, what did it matter? It didn't hurt. As long as you could always get them, and mostly you could. They came to her without an effort, and that meant she was meant to have them, they were a gift of the gods, thank you gods.

She took out her pills. One, then. And she'd get some tea, or she'd die of thirst. She swallowed the pill with some disgusting

131

burning liquid left at the bottom of another cup. What did you do that for? No hope of sleeping any more now. It was only mid-afternoon outside. She couldn't go out yet. She had insomnia of the worst kind: daylight insomnia.

And there was no money, not even enough for some tea. There was only one area in which all her spells failed. She could not make herself rich. She could foretell the future, she could wyrd people, she could conjure up goblins and pacify demons, but she could not create material wealth and comfort for herself. And they would not tell her why.

Eveleen, hoping for some portent, looked around her dingy, scungy room. A deathly stillness. What was that? A canvas splashed with fresh paint. Oh yes, after everyone had finally gone this morning she had done some work. She loved those quiet mysterious hours before dawn: that was when she felt her strongest, that was *her* time. She had done all her best paintings in those magic hours. The Panther. The Covenant. Firebird. Those paintings had captured something of the power that had guided her, and would have their disturbing effect on viewers forever. They were all a few years old, now. Quite a few. Eveleen, why are you thinking of time, of time, of years that pass? You are still an artist, you are still painting, just look at this.

She looked at it, the crude brush strokes, the attempt to reproduce the vivid, pulsating creatures that had leapt out of her past canvases . . . but this messed-up thing was not like that, it was splashed with a crude, lifeless mockery of her vision. What had she been thinking of? Someone had given her money for a painting and she needed the money. Perhaps she could work on it. It only needed . . .

'I have to say,' she said aloud, 'this is not the best thing you have done.' It didn't matter. They'd pay for it, she had painted it, it had her name on it. 'Christ, Eveleen,' she swore, holding onto a chair as she looked at the travesty on the canvas, saw its distinctly crude quality, the single thrusting movement rather than the tantalising meanderings of her earlier works. Their delicacy, detail and intricacy had gone: gone were the suggestions

132

of layers of smoky dreams in smoky shades, of alluring mysteries in softened tones. The garish, murky work she was now looking at was the betrayal of the gifts she had been given. 'Christ,' she said, 'you haven't done anything good in years.'

She stood there, still, in the shock of realising she'd uttered a bitter secret truth.

It wasn't the truth. It was just the coming down. If she was in her normal frame of mind she'd be pleased with her work. Maybe everyone should have to take some speed before they could look at her paintings. Ha ha.

No response. Everything around her was still. No other life was in the room; nothing but its flat physical dimensions existed. She took a deep breath: her breath made clearer her terrible loneliness in that emptiness, that silence.

A silence in which her most ardent invocations would not be heard. *They* came at their will.

A hollow empty silence, a silence without life. Not like that silence in which she had discovered the music of the silent city, her dexedrine symphony.

Then, she hadn't slept properly for fifty, sixty, seventy hours or more. She had been in a trance for two days. She had painted and painted in a frenzy, possessed. When it was over, she went for her walk, her senses sharper than sharp.

I walked around the city streets; there was not another human soul around. It was an hour before dawn. I heard every sound in the city, every breeze, the breathing of sleepers, the stirrings of animals, the electricity in the wires above me, the stretching of the trees to the skies, the dance of leaves on the branches, the pulsating life in every manifest thing. Each sound was preternaturally clear and distinct, and simultaneously each sound was part of a symphony of related sound.

You will write this symphony, you will hear what I hear, your senses will sharpen beyond what you can imagine. You will create music beyond anything you, even you, brilliant maestro, can yet imagine. I will give you this power. Anything you can do now you

133

will do countless times better, you will have the powers of life, of creation, of supreme will.

Where was her symphony? Where was her conductor? She had done all that for him! Oh, yes, he was away. He was abroad. He was buying things for her, for them: books, pictures, masks.

He had better be! In a wave of fury she recollected his trying to tell her that he could not go on with it, that he thought his powers were declining, that he had learnt what he needed and . . . oh, some rubbish, she wouldn't hear of it. She had ordered him to kneel, to submit to the lash, and to renounce all the doubts sent to trick him.

Where was he? She needed some money for tea. She was weak, horrible energies were sucking strength from her. Who was doing this to her? Was it him, over there, far away? She'd find out and put a wyrd on him!

You must be careful with your curses, Evvi, every curse returns to you, returns fourfold . . .

What the hell. She only hexed people who deserved it. That wasn't why she was feeling so sick. A lot of people had deserved it lately; stupid, mean creatures people were. She shouldn't have anything to do with people.

'Should I, dearest, my dearest?' she said, picking up Isis, who mewed painfully. 'Nothing to eat,' purred Evvi. 'I will conjure you some food.' The cat jumped out of her arms and walked a few steps, its tail curved up into an arc of disdain. 'When it's dark, darling,' Evvi whispered. 'This is a terrible hour to be up.'

Her heart was starting to move. She took another pill, and sat on the bed. She needed some magic to raise her spirits, raise her energies, inspire her to create art again. Last night—that nonsense. What was she thinking? Was it nonsense? They had their ritual, her drunken guests; their magic circle cast, demons summoned, a game where the High Priestess flagellated each of them in turn then fucked the chosen one as the others circled them—only way he could get a fuck, she knew that, he had no idea what it was meant to be about. If she had told them the

134

truth, that the Power had not been there, that no Divine Other was channelled through anyone, just a lot of dumb raucous idiots having an orgy . . . oh she was getting careless. Finally everyone left, and no one left anything for her, no gifts, no food, nothing she needed! Who were those people, those hangers-on, come to look and play and take from her? They didn't value her powers, none of them gave her a thing. She was a High Priestess! She'd wyrd them. She needed some good strong magic, a fire to the magickal imagination, a magickal fire, a union with her dear protecting Elemental. If only he were here, her djinn, Eduard.

Eveleen was sitting, starkly still, in a wide-awake stupor on the bed, when Terry crept in. He stood in front of her, and they looked at each other.

Frail, thin Terry: her son, her mate; a waif, a poet, a Peter Pan, who needed her, understood her as she understood him. He was too delicate, too unbalanced to deal with the world; she dealt with it for him. He was the only human being she had endless time for.

He saw her sitting there in a black cloud. He waited for her to tell him why. 'Is this my life?' she asked. Her despair sounded only like a mystery to him. He didn't have a clue. He was pathetic, a bludger, a leech, a parasite.

'Look,' he said, showing the small parcel he carried. 'I got some tea.'

She only stared at him.

'And we'll have a little dexie,' he said helpfully.

24
GETTING AWAY

When he was on the afternoon shift at the paper, Patrick would have breakfast at Mick's cafe on Darlinghurst Road. Hamburger (with an egg and burnt onions).

Peter from the record shop had his head buried in a paper; a couple of working girls were having tea and toast, and at the counter another young woman was paying for what she had had. 'It's three and six altogether,' Mick said, and gave her one of those patient, knowing looks. The girl was fumbling in her purse, counting out pennies and ha'pennies. They were clearly all the money she had, and it wasn't enough. 'I had it before,' she said. 'Someone's taken it.'

Patrick had a good look at her. 'I'll get it, Mick,' he said. She turned round to look at him. 'Hello Julie,' he said. 'I thought it was you. What are you doing here?'

'Patrick Morris. City boy now, eh?' She tried not to show her surprise.

'The usual, mate?'

'Thanks, Mick.'

Julie raised her eyebrows. 'The usual', they said to him, right in the middle of Kings Cross. Not that she was impressed, she told herself.

'You must sit down and have a cuppa with me,' said Patrick, 'tell me how things are back home.'

'Back in Woop Woop!' she said scornfully. 'Don't talk about it. I couldn't wait to get out, now I want to forget about it.' But she sat down.

They had grown up in the same town; she was younger, she'd been a good friend of his little sister for a while.

She hadn't left the way Patrick did; she didn't have a job

to go to, she didn't have anything; they didn't want her to go. She just wanted to get out. You know how it is, Patrick. She was about to get married, just like everyone else, just for something to do. No, not Tig O'Brien, she broke up with him, he got married to Joy Wilson and she's had two babies. Julie was going to get married to Dennis, you know . . .? Yeah, him. Suddenly she thought, I'm only seventeen, he's not such a good catch and I don't want to end up like Mum.

She wanted to go out and have more fun but people back home said mean things about girls who went spreading their scent around. All she could think about was getting away from there. Coming to the city. To Kings Cross, where it was all parties and nightclubs and rich men. She didn't think it would be like this. Anyway, here she was, and she had a room in Victoria Street and was meeting some really nice people. She even got herself a waitressing job the first week, but it didn't work out.

Mick brought over Patrick's hamburger, and two cups of tea.

'Want something to eat?' Patrick offered.

'Nah,' Julie said regretfully. 'I've had some.' She put milk and sugar in her tea. 'There are plenty of coffee shops round here. I'll get another job. I did have the money,' she said, referring to the breakfast, 'but I was robbed. That's Kings Cross. There are thieves and robbers.'

'I've lived up here for two years,' said Patrick. 'Unrobbed.'

'It's all right for boys,' Julie sulked. 'A girl's got to get tough around here.'

He couldn't tell if she was boasting or complaining. He wasn't sure what to say. There must be something wrong with a girl living alone and unprotected in the Cross, but he sympathised with her need to get away from home.

'What's it like getting tough, Julie?' he asked, wondering if he could write a story for the paper on girls coming from the country to the city: their hopes and disappointments, the perils . . .

Julie was unused to questions without built-in answers. 'You got to be,' she whined. Julie wanted to impress Patrick, but she also began to wonder if she could get anything out of him. 'The

types around here, the weirdos. There's crooks, there's a *witch*.
I've seen her,' she shuddered.

'Evvi,' he said familiarly. 'She's harmless.'

Julie stared. 'You haven't met her?'

'Sure,' said Patrick. 'She's an interesting woman . . .' He
realised he was showing off. He decided Julie could take care
of herself and was too dumb to worry about. She depressed him.
He didn't want to think why. Her silly ambitions mocked his
own. He finished his food and lit a cigarette. Seeing her expression,
he gave her one. Smoking, too. Well, why not. If boys can smoke,
girls can smoke. It was a pity it made her look so cheap. That
was a terrible thing to think. He didn't like the thoughts he had
around Julie.

'When you left home,' Patrick asked, 'what did you think
you were going to do?'

She shrugged. 'Be a waitress. But somewhere posh, in a lovely
frock. Somewhere with a band, and roses.' The private imagination
and desire, thought Patrick, of the little girl who lived down the
street . . . 'I wish the war was still on,' said Julie, resentfully.
'My cousin Deanne had a beautiful time in the war and nearly
married an American.'

Peter from the record shop folded his paper and went out,
nodding at Patrick as he passed and glancing at Julie. Patrick
felt a bit embarrassed, though he wished he didn't. How much
had happened since they lived near each other. He had changed.
Did Julie see that?

'You've changed,' said Julie. He was annoyed, not knowing
quite what she meant. 'Working on the city paper now,' she said.
'Is it good? Meet all kinds?'

He shook his head, to indicate he met more kinds than he
could say, more than you can imagine, even you, Julie, with your
pastiche fantasies of the city as one long dizzying night of sweet
music and film stars.

'Sure do,' he said, rather absently. He suddenly had a memory
of Julie and his little sister, years ago, feeding a baby kangaroo
from a bottle, the way they laughed in delight as the little joey

138

sucked hard on the rubber teat, his mother watching them, he watching the whole scene. The sense of his past home came to him with more clarity and force than he had ever felt since he left there. He could ask Julie for all the news from home, if she still saw his sister, who was still there, doing her Leaving Certificate, whom she had last seen there, what they were doing.

But neither of them said another word about back home, back in the bush; they didn't want to open up the memories; they were here to get away from all that, here to be independent adults in the city. One day Patrick would be able to find the value in his early life; but for now, it was as if that town, that past, would reach out and drag him back if he allowed its reality to intrude too far into his new life.

He looked at his watch. 'I've got to go, Julie. Good luck with getting a job. Guess I'll see you if you're going to be around.'

'Where do you live?'

He didn't really want to tell her. 'Just down the road. The landlady doesn't allow visitors. I'm in here quite a lot.'

'Yeah well,' she said. 'I'll see you then.' She forgot to say thanks for paying for the breakfast.

25
SAME OLD STORY

Julie Berger had come to the Cross with her head full of dreams, dreams without shape or plot or character, but full of gaiety and compliments. She would attract attention and laughter and go to endless parties where bubbly sweet things were drunk and strange and beautiful creatures danced around, and she, Julie Berger, would be in the midst of it all. She would become famous for something, people would know her, her name and her face, they would talk about her and want to meet her. Whatever would she be famous for? Julie thought her talents were a sleeping beauty waiting for the kiss of opportunity. To Kings Cross then. She imagined men in hats inside limousines gliding through half-lit streets where artists sat at sidewalk cafes, sipping French things with their models. She would be part of this glamour, and discover what it was she felt so passionate about.

If Kings Cross were not the way she imagined it, the reality of its dimensions easily replaced the fantasies in Julie's mind. Her imagination flared occasionally but was soon dampened.

She found a room, then found another, and soon was exchanging landlord stories with all the other struggling young refugees of the area, whose own ambitions were also as sure as they were undefined. Same old story, been told a hundred times, but she didn't know that.

There were waitress jobs. A girl from her second boarding house told her there was a job at the California, where she worked. Julie got a job, and served ice-cream sodas and hot dogs in the American-style cafe, and began to go to parties. Her enthusiasm for waitressing wore off and one day she found it easier to stay in bed than get up for work. She didn't have a job the next time she showed up there, so she went to see the nice bloke who'd kept her up so late. He told her that her ideas were childish, being a nice girl in the city meant something quite different, and they looked after each other for a while.

So Julie became a bit of a tramp, something she only occasionally admitted to herself. At least she wasn't selling herself on the street for 'short times'. The nice bloke had to go away, and she had another waitressing job for a while, then another man let her stay and took care of things. He wasn't quite as nice, but she thought things would have to turn out all right in time. He lived in a small room—same as she had done—but he did have a big house somewhere that he was going to take her to see one day. Then one day he sent her out for something and she returned to find he'd gone. Their room had been cleaned out. Most of *her* things had gone too. The landlady had taken what was left until the rent owing was paid. Julie was out on the street.

26
WITCHCRAFT FIESTA

Black Magic, a painting by Kings Cross artist Eveleen Warden, was described as 'lewd, lustful and erotic' by Mr Sutherland SM in Central Court today.

The painting depicted a nude woman being embraced by a black panther.

The magistrate was giving a reserved judgement in the case in which John Lawman, manager of the Himalaya Coffee Shop, Kings Cross, had been charged with a breach of the Obscene and Indecent Publications Act by exhibiting pictures by Eveleen Warden.

Mr Sutherland found Lawman guilty and fined him £5.

The other art students pushed in close as one of them read this aloud from the paper. Some of their moans and groans were a mocking punctuation for a stupid legal system that could describe any pictures in these philistine terms. Some of the moans were for pleasure at hearing such a description.

'Who cares what some cheap rag says?' someone said, and walked away.

'No, it's serious. Who is next? What is next? He gets fined for exhibiting these pictures—where does it end? Is it a free country or not? Are we free to paint what we like? Who will exhibit us?'

The art students bought a few flagons of wine and settled down to a heated discussion. Various points of view were put about, some altered, some tossed aside, some ignored.

Most of them had heard of Eveleen, few of them cared about her. No one at art school had ever suggested she was important. But now a cafe owner had been arrested for exhibiting her paintings and the case was taken up as a cause.

All artistic freedom was at stake! Rot, said others, the woman liked stirring, she liked publicity, she courted attention. Anyway, said another, she wasn't a real artist, she with her singlemindedobsessive subjects, her lack of response to either social movements or artistic schools. But we must all be free to paint what we want to, said the first group, and we must also defend the rights of others to paint and to exhibit what they want to. She had an important role, offered someone, regardless of the relevance or merit of her work: an artist's role *is* to challenge accepted notions of propriety, of permissible subjects, of what can be shown. Isn't it funny, someone else said, she has got the kind of notoriety some artists would kill for. While others paint marvellous pictures in desperate obscurity, she is front-page news, an infamous local figure. She made a pact with the devil, suggested another: the devil asked her, does she want to be the best-known artist in Australia, and she said yes yes; many would. Only she forgot to inquire about the devil's conditions: endless police raids, limited talent, and no one game enough to hang her paintings.

And they sprawled over the floor, and smoked endless cigarettes and drank from the flagons, and then realised that Eveleen had given them what they needed. A theme for their end-of-year art students ball! Witchcraft! They would dress up as witches and warlocks and demons and monsters and oracles and familiars and they would paint the walls with signs and symbols and gods and goddesses. A Witchcraft Fiesta!

For some it was a political demonstration, a demonstration of their belief in freedom. Would they ask the press? Would they exhibit pictures at their party, their own, or Miss Warden's, or prints of classics that had been notorious in their time . . .?

For others it was just a good theme for a party. What decorations would they make? What would they wear?

The students collected men's dressing-gowns and black academic robes and decked them with stars, or with the signs of the zodiac. They made papier-mâché thunderbolts and varjas after studying pictures in an encyclopaedia, and carefully painted them. They painted cardboard crowns with crescent moons sitting

143

low on the forehead. They hung the walls with black crêpe paper and pictures of demons and symbols they invented.

They found incense burners and skulls and painted a huge 'Pan, the Horned God' like the one in the newspaper photo of Eveleen.

On the night of the party, they made a fruit punch in a huge vat and poured into it flagons of wine and bottles of spirits. Someone added a few benzedrine pills too. All the tickets to the Witchcraft Fiesta had sold out.

It was Julie Berger's third day without any home at all and she was sick of it. She was sick, full stop. For two days she had slept on the floor of a crowded little bedsit that two girls shared with any friends who needed somewhere to lie down. Their landlady didn't care what they did, as long as the rent was paid. The girls didn't care what their landlady did, as long as they could come and go as they pleased. The place was filthy.

All the girls called themselves waitresses, but most of them usually got by through cracking it on the street. They walked their little lane in East Sydney and took the johns to a house there that allowed casuals like them to use it. As long as they got their cut. It wasn't like really working.

Julie felt quite sick now. She didn't have any money left, after putting in her share for some food and some pills and some booze. She wasn't able to go back to the room that night, too many people had baggsed the space already.

She had gone to the Green Park pub where they let women in the front bar, but had had to get out of there fast. Constable Murphy had come up to her and asked to see her £1/10. If she didn't have a guinea on her she could be arrested for vagrancy. 'My girlfriend's minding my handbag,' she'd said swiftly, moving as if to fetch it as she spoke, and she'd made a dash for the door and kept running.

She sat on an upturned garbage can in a laneway and decided her life was over. She had nowhere to go. She felt sick, a kind of sick that nothing would make better. Nothing she could think of without crying like a baby, and she couldn't do that here. She didn't really have any friends up here, those molls she was hanging around with couldn't do anything for her, all they did was tell her where she could go to crack it for a pound that'd be spent by the next day. She hated it anyway, ugly old codgers having a root, and probably she was pregnant if she thought about it. She couldn't go home, not without new clothes and a much better story than anything she could think of. How would she get back anyway?

She felt that she had been trapped into the wrong life. Nothing had turned out the way it was meant to. She was being punished for all the bad things she had done in Sydney, and she was going to be punished some more, she knew.

She remembered that once, long ago, she had been taught to be good, and had been promised the reward of heaven that had seemed too distant then. She had been warned about being bad, and had been promised punishments that suddenly seemed too close now. It crossed her mind that she might find a priest, but the thought made her feel sicker and more tired than ever. The penances would take far too long, so she might as well go to her eternal damnation right now.

It was getting dark, and there was nothing lying around she could kill herself with. So she got up, kicked the garbage can till it bounced off the brick fences, and wandered up to the Cross.

'Hey Julie,' a girl's voice called out. It was one of those molls from the crowded bedsit. Julie went over to her. 'Coming to the party?' she said.

The little terrace house in Darlinghurst was packed so tight that everyone was nearly on top of each other. Julie was having the most fantastic time. She drank the punch down fast, and started to feel great. Buzz, noise etc. . . . This was the life . . .

'Enjoying yourself?' a man asked her. He was really nice and friendly and went to get her another drink, saying, 'Don't go away.' She waited for him, squashed up against the stair rail, listening to the noise of the party and the wild music from the

145

next room. He pushed his way through the crowd back to her. 'Live around here?' he asked her. Julie started giggling. 'What?' he said. 'I don't need to live anywhere, just go to a party every night,' she said. He laughed, he kept laughing. 'Hear that?' he said to some other people. 'You don't need a place to live if there's a party every night.' They laughed too, and she felt brilliant, beautiful and admired, and drank the glass down very quickly.

'Feel good? You're going to feel extra extra good. Don't go away,' he said, and returned with his hand closed over something. 'Take one,' and he gave her a little pill. She drank it down. He took one too, then broke the third one in half and shared it.

Out in the street it was getting cooler. 'Cold for this time of year.' Julie was in a group going on to some other party. Some art students had a big do on tonight, and once it was this late, way past midnight, all the squares had gone home and you didn't need a ticket any more—you could get in.

Julie moved through the streets, clutching onto the man. She felt she was slipping and would go for long slides, she felt she could walk in the air, she felt she was sinking through the pavement. She hung on tight to him and he hung onto her and they fell down together and she hurt her arm. He was laughing too much to notice.

They had been walking down the same street for hours and hours. Days. Her face was falling apart. Her brain was breaking up into tiny bits and hurtling round inside her head. There were creepie-crawlies all over the fences and monsters lurking round corners ready to pounce. A man was hanging onto her and she didn't know who he was. Some people were going 'oohh oohh' and talking about a witch, *the* witch, it was a witches' party. Jesus, Mary and Joseph. She couldn't recognise the place they were going to. It looked like some kind of old prison, really creepy, big stone walls; they were inside, she felt such a panic, such a fear, and then stood aghast as she saw the devil himself through the doorway inside—she saw that she could never avoid what she had deserved. She couldn't speak, she was so scared, and the man said come on, come on, and pulled her along, and

146

they got to the door and inside was Hell itself.

She turned and ran and ran, crashing into walls and fences, led by blind instinct to Darlinghurst Road, where she was delivered into the arms of a couple of big beefy blokes in blue uniforms.

27
IDENTIFICATIONS

APPEAL UPHELD

In the Quarter Sessions Appeals Court Judge Bailey today told nineteen-year-old Julie Kerryn Berger, formerly of Kings Cross, she was 'capable of saying anything'.

He upheld an appeal by the girl against a two-month sentence for vagrancy, and placed her on a twelve months' good behaviour bond.

On 22 November Det.-Const. H. Idol told Central Court that Berger had said she had been to a 'black mass' at Kings Cross and Eveleen Warden was the 'black witch of the Cross'.

Later Berger denied she had ever been to a 'black mass'.

Berger, a plump blonde, appeared in court today dressed in a black skirt and a tight-fitting silken blouse.

Judge Bailey said: 'I do not place the slightest credence on anything this girl says.

'She is capable of saying anything and involving all and sundry in a good deal of trouble.

'She is publicity mad.'

Judge Bailey made a condition of the bond of £10 that Berger would return to the care of her parents.

Outside the court Berger said: 'All I want to do is live my own life and be a human being.'

I folded the paper and put it down beside the typewriter in front of me. 'Good luck to you, Julie,' I said.

Julie had told the police that she had escaped from a 'black mass' held by the 'witch of the Cross'. Her hysterical, increasingly embroidered stories had set all the papers ablaze with ridiculous stories about satanism and black masses in Kings Cross. I hoped this was the last of it.

I never did the feature on country girls with heads full of

dreams. I had written the ending to Julie's story the same as any reporter would.

The last edition of the paper was out on the street and nearly everyone had gone home. They'd come back late tonight or early in the morning. It was about 3 p.m., the quiet time at the *Daily Mail* offices. I sat there among the acres of close, cluttered desks, in the near-empty office, thinking I should go.

The telephone rang. I picked it up. 'Editorial.'

'I'd like to talk to a very high-up reporter,' said a man's voice, a rough, uneducated voice, a tone of self-importance.

I paused, then I said, 'What can I do for you?'

'I can do a lot for you,' the voice said. 'My mate and I have here a certain property that would be worth a great deal to you.'

'What is that?' I asked. What else could I say?

'It is a film of certain well-known people in very compromising positions.'

'A film?'

'For a consideration,' the voice said in a careful, rehearsed way, 'your paper could have exclusive rights to this film, a scoop. You'd write it up, see, and it'd sell a lot of papers. It's the kind of thing you'd be very interested in. You could publish these pictures with bits blacked out, and let people know what they get up to over there.'

Maybe these blokes had really got something. Maybe this was some kind of chance. 'What is the film about?'

'It's pictures,' the voice said, 'of black magic being practised.'

'Who am I speaking to?'

'Who am *I* speaking to?'

'Patrick Morris,' I said, making it sound confident, important, a name you should recognise.

'Well, Mr Morris, you're speaking to a friend, let's just call it that for now. So would you be interested in it?'

I found Col, bought him a beer, and told him what I'd arranged.

He said he wasn't surprised about the call. He'd been out drinking the night before and had learnt that two men had already

149

rung the other papers, who'd turned them down.

But arranging to meet the men wasn't such a bad idea, he said. You never knew. They'd been knocked back by everyone else, so they'd be more willing to come across and agree to what Col proposed.

Col said he would go to see them. Maybe on his own was best. I agreed with him. No point in my going, I said.

I had no enthusiasm for it. I was busy wondering about life after police rounds. Police roundsman was meant to be a lifelong career. I was meant to be lucky to have got in. And I was. Now I thought I needed some more luck, to get out. Col hadn't liked hearing about the time I had helped prevent some copper mate of his from booking Magda for serving booze outside of the licensing law. Fair enough, he agreed, you look after your mates, but *they* were wogs. 'Friends, eh,' he said, unimpressed. 'Got nothing against them. But you should think about who your friends really are.' And I did.

Col O'Brien bought me a beer and told me the good news and the bad news.

He had met the two men. He'd got the film from them, and told them they'd get their money after, if the film was worth it.

He'd known they would agree to this, because they had nowhere else to go with it. They had been most disgruntled and disappointed to find that no one else had been interested. They had rung the *Daily Post* before they'd got onto me at the *Mail* and had told someone at the *Post* that the pictures were of Evv Warden in a black magic rite and the *Post* had said, 'There's nothing new about that,' and had hung up. Col laughed himself sick. 'Get that,' he said, 'these blokes have got the pictures, they've got the real thing, and the papers have gone to town so much on the made-up thing that they've had enough and don't want to know!'

'These two blokes are a couple of no-hopers,' Col said. 'Couple a' poofs, both been inside a fair bit.' They'd taken to hanging round at the Cross and going round to Eveleen's. They'd stolen this film from her flat.

Yeah, Col had got the pics, the blokes had given him the roll of negatives and he'd got his mate Vince in Photographic to develop them. His mate had made some copies for himself, too.

'Are you ready for this, son?' Col pulled some photographs from an envelope and, grinning, handed them over.

The first one showed a woman, a thin woman, lying stark naked on a high bench, which was covered with cloths so it looked like an altar. Behind her stood a thin naked man, holding an ornate knife aloft, as if he were about to plunge it into her belly. I looked, I saw the woman's bony hips and tuft of dark pubic hair, then I saw that the woman was Eveleen Warden, and the man was that mad young poet who hung around her. I turned to the next photograph. The same woman on the same altar *but* here she had her legs wide open to the camera, and the handle of the knife was protruding from her vagina.

I flicked through the rest of the pictures and handed them back. I kept my composure, I liked to think. It was as much of a test as the morgue and the next of kin had been.

'Jeez mate,' said Col with relish. 'How'd ya like to stick a knife up a sheila's twat?' He disgressed a little to what he'd like to stick up whose what. I swallowed my beer, and waited.

'I took it upstairs,' Col told me, meaning he had gone to see the editor with the pictures. 'But you know the boss, he nearly died, nearly collapsed, he's a strict old tyke, you know, goes to church and all. No, we can't use these.' The pictures were far too shocking to be reprinted, even with blacked-out sections, and anyway the papers had had enough 'witchcraft sex orgies, Eveleen named' stories.

We couldn't use the photos for the paper but Col had other uses for them. The confidence system.

I had been looking at the short stories the paper printed on Saturdays, and was wondering if you could make a living writing those. I was wondering if I could get onto writing the culture

151

page, or the historical feature. I was wondering what you did if you left police rounds.

I bought Col a beer and he told me the latest. His mate Trev from Vice was only too interested.

'Trev asked me, "What's bloody Evvi Warden up to?". I said, "Aw she's up to her antics." He knew there was something up.' Detective-Sergeant Trevor Thomas had a deep dislike of Evvi Warden and her kind. 'He's a straightlaced kind of bloke,' Col explained. 'Nice wife, the kiddies all athletes. He's the clean-cut kind. It really offends him to see those paintings of hers, they put them up in coffee shops. Someone had already rung the Vice Squad about these photographs—someone from one of the other papers. Shouldn't have done it, of course. Confidence is confidence even if it is a pair a' poofs. Your name gets around, no one'll talk to you again. Anyway, Trev knows all about it, and he's keen to pinch them. He had a talk to me about it.'

So Col had told the men to turn up with their film, and he'd buy it off them after all. They'd turned up, and the police had known where to find them. The two had been arrested for possession of pornographic material. You could get twelve to eighteen months for that. One of them was already out on parole, so he was up for a bit more.

'Funnily enough,' said Col, sarcastically, 'they were interested in a deal.'

They'd named names, sworn evidence. Then they'd got six months each.

Detective-Sergeant Thomas now had legal grounds to search Evvi's place. He let Col come along with him. Someone must have tipped her off; she had gone. She hadn't been there for a couple of days. They went in anyway. 'Filthy disgusting place,' Col said. 'A couple of sick-looking mangy cats came rubbing up against our legs. We kicked them away. People who live like that are scum. That devil picture was on the wall. Trev explained it to me. It was a picture of Pan, who was really the Pied Piper from that old story. Apparently the real story was the Pied Piper

152

didn't get paid the first time, when he had taken all the rats out of the town, so he came back and took the children, who were all taken into the white slave trade. Evv and her mob want to do the same, that's why they have that picture up there.' How did he know this? He'd been told by someone who knew someone who had got sucked into their coven for a while. They practised 'pantheism', Col said, disgusting stuff it was.

They had a bit of a look around. Col himself found the bunch of letters, tied together, stuck in an old tin. 'These,' he said to Trev Thomas, 'just might be very useful.'

Col bought me a beer and told me what he wanted.

'I don't get it,' I said. 'He's got worldwide acclaim. He's one of the highest-paid men in Australia. He dresses well, he's had three wives.'

'Yeah,' said Col, 'he's a good style of man, he could have had his pick of women probably.'

'No one in the ABC knew, no one on the north shore knew,' I said, staggered by what I'd heard. 'He really did lead a double life. I don't get it. What was the attraction?'

'The sex,' said Col. 'He was kinky in the sex. When they get like that, they'll do anything to get it, their different forms of perversion. Someone who's normal can go without if necessary, but when they're kinky they get a compulsion. It's a terrible thing.'

I couldn't believe that Col O'Brien really had any valuable insights into human nature, or any idea of the motivations behind the personal proclivities of a man he could never get to know. But I couldn't answer my own question any more satisfactorily.

'So what they need,' Col continued, 'is a positive identification on the letters. He never signed them. Or he signed them some bloody thing, some code. Trev went over to see Nigel Donne, who wouldn't give him the time of day.' Donne was the music critic on the *Mail*. 'Never knew that von Kronen was a particular mate of Donne's, but anyway he wouldn't be in it. Told Trev to see the bank manager and stalked off. Just a thought, mate,' Col said, and I had no idea what was coming. 'How're things

153

going with that little wog girlfriend of yours, the music student?'

I drank my beer. 'All right.'

'Get it in yet?'

I didn't reply.

'Ever the gentleman. If you could get something with the man's handwriting on it, you'd be set for life. You and the coppers—no worries, you'd be trusted for good. New grade. Pick of jobs. Just a thought.'

I thought of the letter Nora had received and shown me proudly, a letter saying she had been accepted into some special class that year. It had a handwritten message and signature from the maestro himself.

'I'd be worried,' said Col, as if he could read my thoughts, 'about any young girl studying under him. They like getting young recruits into these covens of theirs. Trev's heard of a student who was asked to join. I hope it wasn't your girlfriend.'

'No,' I said. 'I reckon not. I don't know if she'd have any signature or anything, but I'll see.' I was wondering if maybe I could get a job on one of the morning papers. How would I go about it?

Evvi's sister had answered the door. It was a neat, decent house on the north side: a fibro house with shiny lino floors. The sister let them in. Eveleen and Terry the Poet were sitting in the neat lounge room, looking out of place and very sick. Eveleen hardly glanced up.

'You'll be coming with us,' Detective-Sergeant Thomas said. He looked around him and felt sorry for the sister. He showed Eveleen what they'd taken from her place, keeping a safe distance, but she didn't even move, just glanced at the bundle.

'Whose letters are these?' Thomas asked.

'That's my personal mail' said Eveleen. 'Where did you get them?'

'Where did you leave them?'

'What were you doing there?'

'Looking for you,' he said. 'That is a filthy place you live in.'

154

Evvi said, 'That's what I'd say about your mind.'

Someone had tipped off the detective, told him where Eveleen was to be found. He told her what charges she was up for, on the evidence he had. He told her what sentences she would receive. She said she'd see her solicitor.

The solicitor got back to him. Funnily enough, Evv would be interested in a deal.

I was interested in a story in the paper that day. *Australian radio is suffering from a shortage of first-class scriptwriters and the position is likely to become even more acute with the development of television*, it said. Perhaps the future held more possibilities than I had yet imagined. *Top writers seek bigger rewards overseas*, it said. *Sumner Locke Elliott, Lindsay Hardy* . . . Maybe there was more to do in the world than I had let myself see so far.

28
THE LETTERS

The letters found by Detective-Sergeant Thomas and Col O'Brien were in an untidy bundle; although they were not well cared for, they had been carefully saved and put aside. The envelopes had not been kept, so there were no postmarks; none of the letters was dated. The pages were unordered and unnumbered; most of them were on air-mail paper, suggesting an overseas origin; one of the notes was on a postcard from France. They had all been written by the same hand: neat and even, with the letter e and d formed like Greek letters: ε and δ.

What a lifesaver you are! The package came today and was pored over in bed—what better place? Your letters are a breath of sulphur to me—what vitality and observation. I'd like to get one a week ... but we artists and creators can't spend valuable time putting purely ephemeral things on paper—excepting in good causes such as ours. I'm sure TER writes a good letter too ...

In detail your photostat drawing and poem *vivid* (thanks for telling me the end) the sailor's effusions astonishingly near the point, at times. A good imagination and obviously he was good material. Though crude, poor chap (an interesting piece of communication of Terry in this connection). The anthropologist drawing the best thing of its kind I've seen for a long time. Human and good draughtsmanship. Without mentioning my name (which you'll never do in any connection, anyway; and that's an order from the High Command), would it be possible for you to borrow his entire collection to show me? Some time in the future? The beasts alone are worth it and his youngsters . . .! It all cheered me vastly.

And of course so did your long letter. Mount Victoria, since reading your stories about it, has taken on a new interest. If you come on Friday (and I'm expecting you any time after 10.30) the bus from Katoomba

You're grand people to take the trouble to come. I'll be alone till 4.30 then I'll be surrounded again. The atmosphere is utterly wrong for our purpose, but anyway I don't think we'll bore each other. How right is your idea of getting both the room and the leisure time to occupy it. Obviously a pied-à-terre is necessary, hidden and private. Fortunately at the end of June I'm a free agent, and virtually everything in the way of meetings will be possible at that time, subject always to the heavy claims on my time and energy arising from my schedule. Since last week's rite, there's no question but that these must be at least weekly. That however will only be regularly possible from June onward. But it's worthwhile and important to wait for. Meantime there's lots we can build up. Yes I'll instruct you in the gimoire. The diagrams are necessarily crude but nonetheless effective, being all from unimpeachable sources. You will be my best— and only—pupil, and I shall appoint you keeper of the seals (you nearly hit the nail on the head about AC and self in your letters). Unfortunately I didn't buy the book but shall . . . it to you next week for lesson one. Can you trace the headdress, illustrated in enclosed, worn at an arts ball (I think in Kings Cross) recently. It's the Ashtoroth crown and is for you and no one else, I'm thrilled about the drawings.

By the way it's needless to remind you to lock everything at 179 when you leave. The photo is good, I will take some snaps on Friday. Remind me. Must stop. Deep emanations the SGs and to you

Evviwitch
The monster package arrived obviously by daemonic angel

carrier (such speed) in the afternoon, and contemplating your hermaphrodite organs in the picture nearly made me desert my evening's work and fly to you by first aerial coven. But, as promised, you came to me early this morning (about 1.45) and when a suddenly flapping window blind announced your arrival I realised by a delicious artificial tingling that you were about to make your presence felt in a very real sense. Seriously, you were very definitely here, and you were doubtless enjoyably aware of what took place. I was in the middle of a rite of A and he had just asked for the 'osculum infame' (which I was about to administer) when you took advantage of my position and administered same to me. A strange, hoofed creature was in the room with us—upper and middle parts female, lower centaur, and a pretty crustacean creature with long milky breasts also appeared—I will draw it for you when I see you. All night I was in sheer s.m. delight and my offerings were, by results, most acceptable to the beings . . . More of this later. Your description of triple s.m. rite (you, T and me) was curious because I was . . . of you both as female (T always comes to me as female) and I was fully present, also in changing forms.

It's hard to resign myself that you're not now coming here but I think it was better so from the economic standpoint. I need your physical presence very much, for many reasons. We have many rituals and indulgences to undertake, quite apart from s.m. And I want to take more photos.

In which connection:

(a) Please ask your neighbour whether the excessive light in the pictures is due to under-exposure or over-exposure (of the film, not you) and tell him to get some 'sets'.

(b) . . .

(f) Am bringing back some masks.

Salaam Evvi
I called the a.m. hoping I might collect the finished Λ.

drawings. Knocked 3 times but alas no answer. Saw a light and key in your door but guessed you were out for a spell. I left the second-hand copy of the 'GB' propped against your door, and hope you found it safely there on your return. I found it at the office after leaving you the other day, have since read it and it confirms all I know of AC. Though exaggerated certain things over much.

I experimented on one of the cakes of lighe (page 64) (not successfully). I hope you will have better luck with the unguent.

I am free for ½ an hour about 11.30 on Wednesday. Mail me a line saying it will suit you both if I call. The 3 greetings go to you in this in haste.

djinn

term 'il magico della s-x' (or what may be referred to as s.m.). His dual nature and build well equipped him to deal with its every manifestation . . . consumingly, and with results—(In this connection in your last letter, I wanted you to mount this 'favourite hobbyhorse' of your still further [delusion]. It is also mine!).

I hope what you witnessed last night (I conclude you were present) entertained you *within its limitations*! I think it wiser—since *prudence* must govern for obvious reasons, all things connected with me, also you—that you retain *till I call chez vous for them* the present two A works . . .

. . . not always 'curiosity proof' in relation to packages! This is *not* so with ordinary mail if marked 'personal' and occasionally changed in the matter of handwriting. It is therefore better to send everything through the mail *save packages* which I will call for when the privilege of that desirable familiarity is accorded me! I am the discreetest of beings, and would never intrude except at pre-arranged times. Since you probably have no telephone and also rest during daytime there are three alternatives for . . . a preliminary meeting

I am en route to Melbourne and leave again Friday 21st for S. You can get me at Menzies during those 5 days (mail quite safe) as I am alone. Please forgive this latter portion of tiresome data, it is practical and necessary. I will abstain from such in future, Lady Evvi. (We will depute others to such chores . . .) Should there be others in your circle of friends who might conceivably resent this future intrusion into their proper sphere I will of course refrain from anything in word or writing they might deem improper. I count on you to be frank with me about this.

You probably received a stupid house-dress the colours of which I liked. Throw it away if it bores you. It may do to paint in. Also a transparent oilskin (which you can wear when it rains if you want!!) will reach you, which we'll need for a ritual later. Oh yes, Rasputin. I knew Yusopov who killed him, he had a flat and a mistress in London, tremendous charm and knowledge for my job in particular. He says Rasputin had a tongue *twice the length* of any normal being. This was the secret of his attraction to women (he was impotent, apparently due to almost constant fellatio by children—trained for this). So, the tongue was probably a more than [adequate] substitute in the d

For the holidays I am airfreighting to you a few cheaper fictional works, which you may not have read. (Don't forget to keep for me those exciting ones you mention in your letter.) Later, in a month's time, I am forwarding important paraphernalia for the coven, unobtainable in A. Unfortunately the Master in Paris passed on a few months back. So no more unguent but his assistant is hopeful to let me have more of this later, together with other material magic. I bring also amusing things for our future 'transvestitualities'! And other things too

160

29
IT'S A TERRIBLE WORLD

Nigel Donne stopped me in the corridor. 'Young Morris? Did I see you at the concert the other night? You like music, do you?'

He had never spoken to me before. 'I do like music,' I said, 'but I don't know much about it.' I was afraid he was going to ask me for my opinion. I would have to admit I liked it all, or else quote Nora.

'You go to a few concerts, do you?'

'I've started to, sir,' I said. 'I go to a few.'

'Come in here a moment, would you?' I followed him to his desk. No one was within hearing distance.

'Police roundsman,' he said, looking at me questioningly. I could see he was dying to ask me something. The combination of my job and my concert-going presented him with a contradiction, one he couldn't decipher, yet one that meant I might be able and willing to tell him something he wanted to know.

'That is my job,' I said. 'I've been on police rounds for over a year. But I want to do something else. I'm interested in . . .' I didn't know what to say. 'Other things too,' I concluded lamely.

'Yes, I see,' he said. 'I suppose you are aware of, how shall I say, certain rumours concerning Eduard von Kronen?'

'Yes.'

'They're after him, aren't they?' Donne asked me. 'O'Brien came here a couple of months ago asking me to identify some handwriting.'

'I heard about that.'

'I told him to go away,' said Donne fiercely. 'What has he done? What's it all about? Is it those pictures?'

Quite a few people around the papers had heard about the

photographs by now, quite a few people had seen them, and quite a few people were repeating rumours that von Kronen was involved. Lots of people knew someone who knew someone who knew someone . . .

'I believe so. Yes. Some connection.' I felt uneasy: I didn't know how much to tell him. I knew that Col and his copper mate, one of the detectives from Vice, had got Eveleen to sign a statement that some letters she had received were from von Kronen. Then she signed some statements about committing buggery. Col had become a bit close-lipped around me lately. I hadn't told him I wanted to go on to other things, but I guess he sensed it. He had dropped a few hints about his own plans but I didn't know the details. 'I don't know for sure,' I told Donne.

'All right,' Donne said. I was getting up to leave. 'Look,' he said, 'I didn't like von Kronen all that much, arrogant he was, and played too many infernal modern pieces. But his private life is his own business.'

'I agree with you, sir,' I said. 'I do.'

'I rang up Sir David,' said Donne. Sir David Solomon was the Chairman of the ABC. 'I said, get a message to von Kronen. Tell him they're onto him, tell him to be careful when he comes back. He obviously didn't believe me, he didn't take it seriously at all. Do you know where von Kronen is now?'

'I don't.' No, I didn't know, but I had learnt many months ago that Col O'Brien knew how to find out where anyone was. And I knew that he was keeping track of von Kronen's movements. And I knew that he wanted to know exactly when von Kronen would be arriving back in Sydney, and that he would find out. 'I don't know,' I said, 'but I think they do.'

'Well,' said Nigel Donne, looking old and tired and bitter, 'I tried. What can I do.' He was silent for a moment and I was about to go. 'Good luck,' he said. 'Go somewhere else, that's the right idea. Come and show me something you've written, something of your own.' He turned to the papers on his desk, and I said, 'Thank you, sir, I will,' and left.

Only a couple of months ago I might even have seen it Col's way. Since then I'd been back home for Christmas. When everyone treated me the same, as if I were the kid who'd left there, I felt like a ghost. I knew I had changed. I had intended to, but it was still an intriguing affirmation. I came back to town and Nora said to me, 'When you were away I realised that I have changed.'

The night after Donne talked to me, I met Nora as usual. We walked down Macleay Street and Wylde Street, and found our place, a quiet private place where we could sit and look at the harbour.

Nora had just begun the first term of her last year at the School of Music. It was going to be a big year for her. She told me a bit about her new classes, and she told me how much she was looking forward to von Kronen's arrival, and to learning all he could teach her. What could I say?

Nora paused and looked at me. 'You're so quiet tonight.'

'Sorry,' I said.

'Don't be sorry. What are you thinking about?'

'About myself.'

She laughed. 'You're not very romantic!'

'Sorry.'

'What *is* it?'

I held her close, cuddled her and kissed her neck, breathed in deep the scent of her hair. She felt so soft and tender. Then she moved away and looked at me questioningly.

'I love you, Nora,' I said.

She waited.

'But . . .?' she asked, with a little apprehension.

'No, no. No *but*. There's something I've been thinking about. It was just an idea at first. Now I know it's what I really want to do. I want to leave, leave here, leave Australia. I want to go to London. I haven't got the money. I don't think I'd get a job with the paper over there, they wouldn't send me there, not yet. I'd have to save up, and just go, then get a job over

163

there. On a London paper. Fleet Street. Or the BBC. I'm *going to go*,' I said, for the first time. 'I'm going to aim to go by the end of this year. I'll go to London, and you'll go to Paris. We can't stay here.'

We hugged and kissed. We talked about making this come true. Sadness, excitement, happiness, fear. And what about us? We would go on, as we were, until we left, and then, then what? We didn't know.

Momentous.

'Tomorrow,' she said, 'a group of teachers and students from the school are going to the airport to meet von Kronen.'

'Don't you go,' I said. She looked at me, wondering. 'Just don't go,' I said.

'Why not?'

So then I told her what I knew. I told her what I suspected was going to happen at the airport.

She would never do her Master Class with von Kronen, never get nearer her inspiration, never find her Paris in Sydney.

She cried a bit and I felt like crying too. We sat there, with our arms around each other, and looked at reflections in the vast dark waters, their promise and their treachery; at glimmering lights in the shadows: endless blessings and endless betrayal.

'Why are people so awful?' she whispered, leaning against me. 'It's a terrible world.'